The setting is the fishing village of Strathquinnan on the west coast of Scotland, an island-studded area of rugged beauty. The principle cast is the local lifeboat crew who carry out their rescue missions, sometimes successfully, but at other times, unsuccessfully.

The story is one of bigotry and compassion, of duplicity and heroism, as adultery and crime mingle with the raw, naked courage of the lifeboatmen, all set against a background of complex human relationships and religious tensions in the rather claustrophobic atmosphere of the West Highlands of the 1950's.

Fact merges with fiction as the impact of the loss of the Broughty Ferry lifeboat with its crew of eight in 1959 is felt throughout Strathquinnan. The lifeboatmen and their families catch a glimpse of the crushing blow such a tragedy brings to a close-knit community not unlike their own.

ROCK AND TEMPEST

A NOVEL BY
Webster Simpson

ISBN 0 9538690-4-0

Published by
Itelsor Ltd
Trendell House
3 Lintrathen Street, Dundee DD5 8EF
Tel: 01382 825629 Fax: 01382 832316

Eternal Father, strong to save,
Whose arm hath bound the restless wave,
Who bidd'st the mighty ocean deep
Its own appointed limits keep:
O hear us when we cry to Thee
For those in peril on the sea.

O Christ, whose voice the waters heard,
And hushed their raging at Thy word,
Who walkedst on the foaming deep,
And calm amid the storm didst sleep:
O hear us when we cry to Thee
For those in peril on the sea.

O Holy Spirit, who didst brood
Upon the waters dark and rude,
And bid their angry tumult cease,
And gave, for wild confusion, peace:
O hear us when we cry to Thee
For those in peril on the sea.

O Trinity of love and power,
Our brethren shield in danger's hour;
From rock and tempest, fire and foe,
Protect them wheresoe're they go:
Thus evermore shall rise to Thee
Glad hymns of praise from land and sea.

William Whiting, 1825 - 1878

Chapter 1

"Boom!"

Across the rooftops of Strathquinnan, the sound of the lifeboat maroon reverberated. After the rocket detonated high above the village, its long-decaying echoes returned from the surrounding hills. Even with the howl of the hurricane-force winds and the machine-gun rattle of hail on the window, the dramatic crash shook Morag McLean from the depths of sleep into wakefulness.

"Dod, the boat!" she gasped, still not properly awake. She reached across the bed to rouse her husband, but he was not there. Pulling herself up the bed, she reached for the light and, switching it on, saw Dod, already half dressed, struggling into his trousers. George McLean, Dod to all who knew him, had been part of the Strathquinnan lifeboat crew for over six years and, even when the maroons were fired at dead of night, he was fully dressed before he was fully awake. It took him only a couple of minutes to finish dressing. Then he dashed down the narrow, cobbled street to the lifeboat shed. Morag was not far behind.

Across the road and slightly farther from the shore, Dr Anderson pulled on his dressing-gown and went to the

1

window. He was at the window within seconds of the bang of the rocket but it seemed every light in every home in the village was already on. Less than a minute later the first running steps could be heard. What never ceased to amaze him was where so many people came from within seconds of a lifeboat maroon being fired. The street was soon alive with old and young, men and women, all heading for the boat-house. The elderly doctor had witnessed this scene many times before and did not share the compulsion to rush to the boat shed. As the crowd hurried past, he looked back up the road and, to his horror, he saw the slim and energetic form of the new parish minister sprinting towards him down the street. Anderson thrust open his front door just in time to intercept the young man.

"For goodness sake, man! What do you think you're doing? Come in here this instant!" Without giving the clerical gentleman time to think, the doctor grabbed his arm and pushed him bodily into the house.

"Good grief man! Don't they teach you anything practical at college? If those lads there had seen you, no doubt they'd still have launched the boat because they're brave lads, but none would expect a safe return. Don't you know that the whole crew of a fishing boat have been known to go back home rather than put to sea after meeting a minister in the street on their way to the harbour? Superstition you probably call it, but it's very real to them and perhaps even more so to their families. However, I don't think anyone recognised you so there's no harm done."

"Boom!" A second rocket soared into the sky just as

yet more folk ran down the street, so many that, even indoors, the sound of running feet could be heard above the violence of the storm. Dod reached the boat-house to find that the coxswain and the mechanic were both there before him. As if by magic, a crowd of willing helpers appeared and the huge doors at the sea-ward side of the shed were rolled back. More running feet. Several men surged into the boat-house. The coxswain nodded to one and then another and each speedily and silently donned oil-skins and life-jackets. Nimbly the men scrambled on to the throbbing decks of the waiting boat, throbbing because the engines were already ticking over, filling the shed with a dull rumble and a strong smell of exhaust fumes. The coxswain positioned himself behind the huge wheel. Six others crouched in the cockpit beside him. He nodded wordlessly to the local lifeboat secretary who, in turn, waved to a man out of sight under the stern of the boat. There was a warning cry which was followed by a loud bang as the securing-pin which was the last link restraining the boat on the steep slip was knocked out with a single blow from a mallet. With a deep, growing rumble the craft accelerated down the slip-way, its blue and red hull momentarily lit by the flood-lights above the high doorway as it flashed past. The tide was well out and the boat continued to gain speed until its bows smashed through the surf, throwing a colossal wave right over the craft. The water had scarcely cleared from the deck before two of the crew were forward, raising the mast and the funnel. For a few brief minutes the boat's lights could be seen flickering in the darkness. Then the red and green port and starboard lights disappeared in the gloom, leaving only the mast-light visible to the watchers on the shore. Then it, too, was lost in the rain and the spume.

In the now empty boat-house the lifeboat secretary stood apart from the few others who were left there. For all that David McPhail, solicitor, town-clerk and the honorary secretary of the Strathquinnan lifeboat had witnessed dozens of launches in his twelve years of service, he never failed to be deeply moved as he watched men race to be first at the boat, desperate that they should be among the happy few who would be chosen to endure cold and fatigue, danger and hardship in the ensuing hours. McPhail looked round at the disappointed men who had been too late, some by mere seconds - men who were now free to go home to dry homes and warm beds, but who were so reluctant to do so. McPhail, too, was now free to go. He had fulfilled his duty. In theory, he had authorised the launch, even though in reality, he had been far too choked up with emotion to trust himself to utter a word. Besides, he could not imagine what would happen if he ever tried to prevent a launch!

The small crowd of helpers and on-lookers were dispersing and, when McPhail saw an opportunity to slip unnoticed out the door, he did so, holding firmly on to his hat as he left the shelter of the building. With the wind-swept rain dashing into his face, he disappeared into the darkness. There was nothing now for any of them to do but to wait. And waiting was the hardest part.

In an unlit window at the doctor's house, the minister and doctor stood side by side, watching the drama unfold.

"I'm sorry if I seemed rude, but these old superstitions really matter to these people. And it's not just the crew you've to think of. There's the wives and sweethearts, the parents and the children. They've enough to worry about in the coming hours, without a special sense of doom hanging over them!" the doctor said.

"I'm sorry. I didn't know. Or rather, I had of course heard of that kind of old superstition, but I thought it was a thing of the distant past. I felt it was my duty to be seen to be there when the boat went out. What I'd really like to have done was to take some of the bystanders back to the church to pray for a successful mission and a safe return."

The kindly old doctor looked with warm affection at the earnest young man, so keen to make a spiritual impact on the community that was now his parish. If asked if he himself were a pillar of the church, Dr Anderson was wont to reply in Winston Churchill's words. "No! Rather more a flying-buttress. I support the church from the outside!" For all that, he liked what he had seen of the new man at St Columba's. He had long seen himself as being, not just the local medicine-man, but also as an encourager of anyone who wanted to do something positive for the community. And he knew that Strathquinnan needed all the encouragement it could get. The doctor had come to the village soon after his own discharge from the Medical Corps in 1919. He had had a hard first year, as the Spanish flu epidemic had swept the land, adding to the horrendous death-toll of the recent war. After that had come the recession years, during which real financial hardship had hit the town and, particularly, its fishing community. Then the Second World War had cut another swath through the young of Strathquinnan. All too many of the promising young men that Anderson had helped bring into the world in his early years in the town now lay in military cemeteries in Europe, Africa and Asia. Not a few had only the depths of the ocean for their grave. Yes! Strathquinnan needed all the encouragement it could get.

"The men on the boat will be too busy to worry over much as long as the mission is on. It's their folk at home that do the worrying. Each has her own way of coping with the stress, no doubt, but I sometimes wonder if the wives are not as great heroes as the men," he said to the minister. "When you really get to know them, you'll see what I mean."

Chapter 2

The Strathquinnan lifeboat, the 'Florence', surged through the water and the lights of the town soon disappeared from view. For all that the sea was rough in the immediate vicinity of the boat-house, it was calm there compared with what was to come. Strathquinnan and its harbour were sheltered by a long, low-lying island called Eilean Sgreadan which lay more than a mile offshore to the west. Its presence prevented the town from feeling the direct force of any of the Atlantic gales that were such a frequent feature of the winter months. For all that, however, the waves swept round both ends of the island causing an ugly jabble of water which was difficult for any boat to negotiate as it put out to sea.

Five of the seven-strong crew were aboard without having the least idea where they were bound for or what their mission was. There had been no time for questions and explanations prior to the launch. However, it was enough for them that there were people in danger somewhere out there who needed their help. Now, however, the coxswain, shouting to make himself heard above the howl of the wind, told them what he knew.

"There's a Royal Navy gun-boat on the Torran Rocks.

The Navy are sending a destroyer. Why, I don't know! It'll never get near the rocks, or, if it does, it'll end up a wreck itself. The Oban lifeboat's been launched and will be well on its way by now. It's of course somewhat nearer than we are, but, with the wind in their teeth, they'll be hard pressed to make much headway. Seems likely we'll be there a couple of hours before them."

The Torran Rocks! These jagged reefs off the south-west shore of the island of Mull were respected, or, more accurately, feared by all who sailed these waters. These were the rocks made famous in Stevenson's 'Kidnapped' as the reefs on which the ship carrying the kidnapped David Balfour to America foundered. That, of course, was fiction. The fact is that the Torran Rocks have through the centuries claimed innumerable ships and lives.

"The Torran Rocks!" exclaimed Dod. "The poor devils will have little chance, I'm afraid. That gun-boat'll have a wooden hull. Those things are made for speed, not strength. It'll be smashed to match-wood long before we get there!"

"Perhaps. Or perhaps not," the coxswain yelled back at him. "If she ran aground high enough on the rocks when the tide was at its highest, she may still be stuck there above the level of the waves. The tide's still on the ebb so there might just be a chance she'll hold together long enough for us to do something. There's also the slim hope that even if she does break up, survivors can hang on to the rocks. We might get there in a couple of hours, perhaps less. When we round Iona, the wind'll be right on our stern and we'll let it drive us as fast as it will. At that, we'll be there before first light, which may be a problem in itself. It'll be difficult finding her and even worse trying to hold station if we have to wait for daylight."

The lifeboat had now rounded the southern tip of the Eilean Sgreadan and, losing the shelter that the island had hitherto provided, 'Florence' started to buck and skew her way through the great Atlantic rollers which creamed around it. One giant wave crashed over the boat, driving it deep down in the water and carrying away the mast. With it went the radio aerial, so all links with the land or with other vessels were lost. Conversation aboard was now virtually impossible. The wind howled mercilessly round the cockpit, blowing the top off each wave and sending a constant stream of freezing water on boat and men alike. The seven huddled down, getting as much shelter as they could, each conserving his energy, each with his own private thoughts about what might await them at the Torran Rocks.

Chapter 3

Strathquinnan was a fairly typical fishing village. Boats had used the shelter in the lea of Eilean Sgreadan since Viking times. In the 17th and 18th centuries, fishing on a very small scale had been one of the ways that some of the hardy people of that part of Scotland had fought for a living. However, it was the infamous 'Clearances' of the latter part of the 18th and early part of the 19th centuries that had led to the development of the village. Crofters whose forebears had farmed the Highlands since time immemorial were forced off their land by landlords who wanted to make way for sheep. Their homes destroyed, they had been compelled to live on the coast. Understandably their dwellings there were hurriedly and poorly built. Most of the houses were single-storey cottages built of roughly-hewn local stone and roofs of thatch. Many had now been re-roofed with corrugated iron and, in a few cases, with slates. The small harbour was still the focal point of the village, although not its heart. If it had a heart, that was the village square, surrounded by a handful of shops on two sides, the Royal Hotel on the third and, on the fourth, standing high above the other buildings on a grassy knoll, the parish church.

The oldest houses, and the poorest, were those close to the harbour. These, low-roofed and with very small windows, were built gable-end on to the sea. Some few were detached, but most were built in terraces on cobbled streets, all of which radiated out from the square and ran down to the sea-front at or near the harbour. The farther from the harbour, the better was the quality of housing, with larger cottages giving way to the Victorian villas which stretched round the outer perimeter.

Whilst the 'Florence' crawled past Eilean Sgreadan and battled her way round the Island of Mull, the women-folk of Strathquinnan were preparing themselves for the anxious hours ahead and the long, wearing business of waiting. As the doctor had said, each had her own way of coping.

Morag McLean had been only minutes behind her husband as he rushed from their home to the boat-house. Pulling the cottage door behind her, she had put her head down and headed into the mixture of driving rain and sleet that swept the sea-front in squalls. She had joined the small group of women who were huddled in the lee of the boat-house. Shouting to make themselves heard above the wind, they exchanged greetings and waited anxiously to know who were chosen to crew the 'Florence'. There would, of course, be the coxswain, Donald McLeod, the tough 39-year-old who had been on the crew since he returned from the war twelve years ago. Five years of, first Atlantic, then Arctic, convoys meant he knew all that was to be known about the weather conditions that could be expected in January on Scotland's wild, western shores. The years since the war he had spent in fishing, at first with the trawlers sailing out of Mallaig. Since his marriage to Ishbel, however, he had worked on his own, fishing for lobsters. Ishbel had not been at the boat-house as the couple had two young children.

Then there was Thomas Ross, only no-one, except his school teachers, had called him Thomas in living memory. Tam Ross was the marine engineer whose untidy yard was at the far side of Strathquinnan harbour. He was the lifeboat mechanic. Eight years in the Navy, servicing the engines of almost everything from motor torpedo boats to cruisers had given him a sound grounding in every conceivable kind of marine propulsion. His wife, Sheena, was not at the boat-house, her place being at home with four-year-old Sarah.

McLeod and Ross were automatically on the boat every time it answered a shout. The rest of the crew would be made up of the first qualified volunteers to reach the boat-house. Discussion among the women revealed that the brothers Hugh and Charles Fraser were aboard. Their mother was there at the boat-house. She was a prematurely old woman whose husband had been lost on the 'Hood' when the 'Bismarck' had sent it and virtually everyone on board to the bottom of the Atlantic. A little aloof, she stood silently among the rest of the women. Life had been hard for Anabelle Fraser and now the two people in the world who mattered most to her were sailing off into an Atlantic storm. Beside her was Irene McGregor, an attractive, dark-haired young woman who was engaged to her older lad, Hugh.

The rest of the crew were identified as Alistair

Stewart, (Al to his friends), Alexander (Eck) Nairn and, of course, Dod McLean. The women stood around for a few minutes then, one by one, dispersed. Anabelle Fraser and Irene McGregor walked side by side up the cobbled street, parting at Irene's door. Irene went into the cottage, whilst Anabelle went on up the street and climbed the knoll on which the parish church was built. The church was never locked, so she entered, found a light switch and slipped into the family pew where she worshipped Sunday by Sunday, as had her parents and grandparents before her. Irene might have wished to have joined her, but her own parents were staunch Free Presbyterians and Irene could only guess at the row that would follow if it emerged that she had been praying in a Church of Scotland building.

* * * *

Morag hurried back home on her own, pausing only to knock on old Mrs Nairn's door to let her know that Eck was off on the boat. Eck himself was 42. That was generally known. However, no-one knew how old his widowed mother was. She seemed always to have been an old woman, crippled with arthritis. She had never been tall, but in recent years, had seemed to shrink even more, her little world revolving round caring for her son. She would sit, sleepless, by the fire awaiting her son's return.

Once back in her own home, Morag opened the cupboard under the sink. Behind the packet of soap powder was the bottle of bleach. Behind the bottle of bleach was the tin of Zebo for blackening the grate. Behind the Zebo was what she was looking for. A bottle of gin! It was about three-quarters full. It would help her through the waiting hours and by dawn it would be well-nigh empty.

*　　*　　*　　*

Alistair Stewart's young wife, Elizabeth, more commonly known as Lizzie, walked up the road with her brother-in-law, Ewan. She was a sultry, well-endowed woman whose good looks were somewhat spoiled by a permanently disgruntled expression. Ewan, a bachelor, was the local butcher. Although, like his brother, Al, he had gone out in the fishing boats with their father when he was younger, Ewan had settled for life ashore. His war service had been in the army, making him almost unique in a community whose men more normally served either in the Royal Navy or the Merchant Navy. The two reached the fisherman's cottage that was home to Al and Lizzie.

"Come on in and keep me company, Ewan. I'm chilled to the marrow. Stir up the fire and I'll put the kettle on."

Thinking of his own cold and draughty cottage whose fire would by now be out, Ewan followed her into the house. While she made the tea and some toast, he knelt down and blew into the embers of the fire, feeding it with dry kindling and then logs. Soon he had a goodly blaze sending sparks up the lum. The cottage had but the one room, with a small kitchen off it. The room was, however, quite large enough to accommodate a table and four chairs, two easy chairs on either side of the fire and, in a recess, a double bed. The two sat down by the fire and warmed themselves internally with tea, externally in the glow of the crackling timber. Once warmed up Lizzie stood up and shuffled out of her coat, revealing that she was still wearing only a rather skimpy night-dress underneath. Ewan stood up to go.

"There's no need to go unless you really want to, Ewan. Eck won't be back for hours. I'm slipping back into bed. Why not keep me company?" So saying, she switched off the light, leaving the room illuminated only by the blazing fire, sat down on the bed with an inviting smile and swung her long legs revealingly on to it.

* * * *

Across the street in the three-roomed cottage she shared with her father and mother, Irene McGregor had had a late supper with her parents and was trying to settle down for the night.

Sleep, she knew, would be elusive. Hugh, 'Shug' all his life to all except his school-teachers, was somewhere out there, heading into the wild weather of the Minches. Over recent months, they had really got to know each other and there were no secrets between them. She knew just how frightened he was, going out on a night like this. This, she thought, is real courage, not fearlessness, but being scared stiff, yet still putting to sea. Tears welled in her eyes as she thought just how much she loved him.

Irene eased her bedroom door open. Her parents were safely in bed and the house was in darkness. She gently closed the door and opened a drawer full of her summer clothes. From deep inside it, she drew out a book, its identity concealed by a brown paper cover. Her cousin had given it to her last summer when she came from Glasgow to stay for a few days of holiday. One could buy such a book in a city like Glasgow, but not in a West Highland town like Strathquinnan. Instinctively knowing what her stern father's reaction to this book would be, she had managed to keep it hidden, often reading late at night. Tonight she read a couple of chapters. Then suddenly she heard her mother's foot-step. She pushed the book under the bed-clothes and grabbed the old black-covered Bible that lay beside the bed. She opened it at random, only just in time as her mother entered the room.

"You can do the lad no good, sitting there worrying," Mrs McGregor said. "It's the Sabbath tomorrow and you'll be falling asleep in church for sure if you don't get your rest now."

"Aye! You're right enough. I find it so difficult to settle when the boat's out. I'll just read a few verses and then try to sleep."

Once Mrs McGregor had shut the bedroom door again, Irene dropped her eyes on the open page in front of her. "Cast all your cares on Him; for He careth for you." She switched off the light and slipped under the blankets. Surprisingly, she was asleep two minutes.

*   *   *   *

Dr Anderson and Mike Dixon, the minister, sat by the fire drinking tea, following an impromptu supper. Eventually, the younger man said, "Goodness! It's nearly four and I've two services tomorrow. I really must try to get some sleep. Thanks for the supper, but I must get home now."

"I'll not sleep readily myself, but I'm an old man now. I don't need the sleep I once did. I'll walk you up the road. The fresh air'll do me a power of good." So saying, the doctor pulled on his coat and the two went out into the wind and the rain.

As they neared the church, Dixon said, "There's a light on! I'm sure the building was in total darkness when I came out."

"That'll be Mrs Fraser. Her two lads are away out on the boat. She'll be there until they're safe in harbour again."

The two men quietly opened the door at the back of the church. In the dim light they could make out the hunched form of the widow, absolutely static in her pew. Dixon made as if he would go over to her, but the doctor pulled him back.

"Leave her be," he whispered. "She's not alone. Her God is with her. She'll be all right and you'll only embarrass her. I tell you, they each have their own way of coping. Just let her be."

Chapter 4

By four in the morning, the 'Florence' had cleared Iona and had turned her stern to the wind. By now it had eased somewhat, but was still at least force five. Huge Atlantic rollers threatened to poop the boat as she ran before both wind and waves. In less time than they had expected, the crew found themselves off the Torran Rocks. Farther out to the south-west were the riding lights of a large ship which was moving slowly eastwards. As the lifeboat moved in towards the white surf that creamed over the rocks, a signal light started to flicker from the ship behind them.

"That'll be the destroyer. What're they saying?" demanded Tam.

McLeod, whose experience on the convoys had left him with a better than average working knowledge of signals, said "'U'! They're keeping on sending 'U'. It means 'You are standing into danger.' As if we didn't know! That's what we're here for! Give me that Aldis lamp."

The next few minutes saw an interchange of signals.

"Right!" said McLeod. "We're half a mile too far west. They're going to fire star-shells. Once we've sighted the wreck, they'll dump oil to sea-ward of us. Keep your eyes peeled and get the rocket lines ready."

'Florence', still pitching and tossing despite the moderating wind, eased closer to the reefs and worked her way eastwards. Suddenly the whole scene was flood-lit as a star-shell from the destroyer soared heavenwards. Dazzled by the glare, the seven men all peered through the rain and the spume, trying to locate anything in the maelstrom that swirled over and around the rocks. As the light of the first flare started to fade, another shot upwards to bring new intensity to the light over the reefs. Suddenly, through the spray, the dark mass of the gun-boat's hull could be seen for a second, before another wave crashed over it.

"Well! There she is," shouted McLeod. "Whether there's anyone left alive on her is anyone's guess. The wind's easing off. The storm may have blown itself out, or could be we're just in the eye of it. Either way, we've a chance. Not a great one, I grant you, but a chance. We'll hold off until we see some sign of life, then we'll try and get a line aboard her."

So saying, he turned and signalled rapidly to the destroyer that was now almost motionless in the water half a mile off. The response was immediate. A signal flashed back. "Received and understood. Wilco." The destroyer surged forward and swept round dramatically towards the reef, continuing in its arc until its bows were headed westwards and it was running parallel to the raging waters crashing over the line of rocks. It passed a mere two hundred yards away from the lifeboat.

"They're dumping oil. We'll hold off for a few more minutes then I'll take her in closer."

They smelled the oil before they saw its effect, but when it was washed towards them the resulting calming of the water had to be seen to be believed. To seaward of the lifeboat, the rollers lost their white caps and visibly flattened off. As the oil reached the 'Florence', the lifeboatmen choked on the strong diesel-oil fumes which wafted around them. Then, beyond them, the white breakers on the reef also started to abate, the seas heaving in an unreal sort of calm. The star-shells continued to burst in the sky above them and the wreck was now clearly visible. The gunboat's bows were high up on a rock, but the stern had been smashed to pieces. Of the vessel's eighty feet, fewer than fifty remained visible, the rest being either shattered by the force of the waves or being under water.

"Fire off a flare and let's see if there's any response."

Seconds later, a bright green flare shot from the lifeboat up into the sky over the wreck. As it died, a red flare rose from the stricken gun-boat.

"Well! Thank the Lord! There's someone alive! Look lively, now! We'll close with the reef. Dod! See if you can shoot a line over her."

Easing the throttles open, McLeod spun the wheel to port and the boat closed the gap between it and the wreck, reducing it to about fifty yards. Standing as steadily as he could on the heaving boat, his back braced against the cockpit coaming, Dod aimed the line-carrying rocket and fired. However, as he did so, the craft lurched and there was a heavy thump from below the keel. The rocket shot out and thumped against the hull of the gun-boat just above the water line, falling uselessly into the water below.

"Missed! Blast! Hold her steady and I'll try again."
He aimed once more. This time the rocket soared over the
bows of the gun-boat and the line fell flat across the fore-
deck. Someone aboard the wreck grasped the light line and
soon a heavy warp was being pulled over from the lifeboat.
Meanwhile, an ominous grinding could be heard under the
lifeboat's keel.

"We'll have to get clear before the oil disperses. Hold
the wheel while I signal the Navy."

Dod eagerly grabbed the wheel and McLeod started
blinking out his message to the destroyer. Seconds later, the
reply flickered from the naval vessel's bridge.

"They're going to make another pass dumping more
oil. That should buy us just about enough time to get the
survivors off and back into deep water."

By then, the two Fraser brothers had rigged a
breeches-buoy and it was swung out over the side. The
watchers on the wreck started to pull it in. Then, one by one,
the survivors were hauled across the oily water, sometimes
above it, often under it. Eager hands pulled them to safety on
to the slippery decks of the waiting 'Florence'. McLeod
scrambled through the hatch to join Tam Ross, the mechanic,
in the engine room.

"Well. What do you reckon? We hit fairly hard. Is she
holed?"

"A plank or two stove in alongside the keel, I'm
thinking. She's making water in the fore-cabin but, with any
luck the pumps will hold her."

"I'd better take a look," replied the coxswain and the two men slithered forward to the cabin where several inches of oily water washed to and fro across the floor.

Another huge wave lifted the craft and slammed her down hard on the rock.

"That'll be another plank gone, I'm thinking." said McLeod grimly. "We'd better get the boat out of here fast."

By the time he reached the cockpit, the last man had been taken off and was lying on the cockpit floor retching.

"The poor devil went right under and has swallowed a puckle more diesel than is good for him," said Dod, as he yielded his position behind the wheel to the coxswain.

"Do what you can for him. Better get them all below. We're putting out to sea again and it'll be fell rough once we get out of the oil."

The cockpit was now slippery with oil and McLeod struggled to keep his feet as he swung the wheel hard to starboard and opened both throttles wide. 'Florence' trembled as the twin screws bit the water and then the boat started out towards the open sea. The destroyer's light started to blink again. McLeod nodded to Al, who slipped behind the wheel, leaving the cox free to reply. He made "All safe. All well. Heading for Oban."

The 'All well' part of his signal was perhaps more optimistic than accurate. In the fore-cabin, the eighteen wretched survivors were all retching, huddled into the tiny space. All were soaked to the skin, were coated to a greater or lesser extent in oil and were shivering uncontrollably with cold. Most had swallowed a sea-water and diesel-oil cocktail and were trying to cough it up again. However, all were alive. A mixture of water, oil and vomit sluiced to and fro across the floor. At least the pump did seem to be holding, for the level was tending to fall. The smell of diesel was nearly overpowering.

'Florence' made good time considering the conditions and, half an hour or so later, came up on the Oban lifeboat which was gallantly punching its bows into the wind and waves, trying hard but making little more than five knots. McLeod signalled. "Radio gone. Taking water. Pump's holding. 100% survivors. Please inform Strathquinnan." Back came, "Received and understood. Will escort you."

As the two boats ran before the waves on their eastward course, the watery, grey light of dawn picked out the dark mass of the Island of Mull to the north. In growing daylight, they entered the Firth of Lorne, increasingly coming under the shelter of the island. The swell abated as they passed Kerrera, the small, low-lying island that screens Oban harbour from the full fury of Atlantic weather. Weary, but immensely satisfied, the men of Strathquinnan, made fast at the pier and transferred the survivors to a waiting bus which had been provided, unasked, by the local transport company. It whipped them all off to the hospital.

Although it was only just after nine on a Sunday morning and the wind and rain were still making life very unpleasant, it seemed as though the whole population of Oban had turned out to see their lifeboat's return. The Oban boat's crew crowded round the Strathquinnan men, pressing invitations of hospitality on them. McLeod gave leave for all but Tam Ross to go and seek food, dry clothing and rest. Then the mechanic and he, aided by two of the Oban crew, took 'Florence' to the boat-repair yard and arranged to have her slipped. There was no question of being able to sail her back to her home station. That was why, eventually, early in the afternoon her crew rather ignominiously returned home to Strathquinnan by bus.

Chapter 5

Irene McGregor awoke with something digging painfully into her ribs. Pulling herself up, she realised she had drifted off to sleep with the brown-paper covered book still under the covers beside her. Daylight was filtering weakly through the windows but no-one else in the house seemed to be astir. Quickly she read another chapter. Feeling she was pushing her luck, she slipped out of bed and concealed the book once more. She might just weather the storm that would surely ensue if she were found reading such a book during the week, but, if her father found her with it on the Sabbath, she would probably have to leave home!

It was now late enough for her to be able to get dressed without it being an unseemly time to be about on a Sabbath morning. With due care, she put on the long black dress which was mandatory for a young woman attending a Free Presbyterian church. When she went through to the kitchen, she found her mother alone.

"Your father's just taking a step outside to get a breath of fresh air. He'll be back presently."

Irene smiled a secret smile to herself. The old man would not have anything as worldly as a wireless in his home, still less would he dream of listening to one on a Sabbath day, even to hear the latest news. However, he would almost certainly meet some less scrupulous member of the community who would have listened to the BBC Home Service news that morning. Without feeling the least bit hypocritical, McGregor would learn what the latest on the lifeboat was as he took his breath of fresh air.

Sure enough, the old man walked back in just a few minutes later. "We must thank Almighty God for the mercies he has vouchsafed to the men of Strathquinnan. The lifeboat has rescued all the survivors and is expected to anchor at Oban within the hour."

To her embarrassment, Irene burst into tears. Her father looked on with a mixture of surprise and perplexity. Having steeled himself to expect nothing but constant suffering in a world that he always described as 'this vale of tears', he had little understanding or empathy with his less stoical daughter.

*   *   *   *

Across the road, Ewan Stewart had cautiously let himself out of his brother's home an hour before dawn, returning to his own cold and miserable little house. Lizzie was sound asleep when he left and looked set to sleep for hours yet.

*   *   *   *

Ishbel McLeod had hardly slept a wink. She tossed and turned restlessly, all the time wondering what was happening on the lifeboat. Her husband, Donald, had so much experience behind him, both in the Royal Navy and on the lifeboat, that she was totally confident that, if anyone could help the poor souls on the Torran rocks, the men of Strathquinnan led by her coxswain husband could and would. But she also knew all too well the awful danger of those Torran Rocks.

Unable to sleep, she rose early. Her two children were sound asleep so she hurriedly dressed and left the house silently. She walked the few steps to Anabelle Fraser's cottage. Ishbel knew that there was no chance of finding the old lady at home. So long as her boys were out on the boat, Mrs Fraser would be in the church. She also knew that the untended fire in the cottage would be long-since out, leaving a miserably cold home for Mrs Fraser to return to eventually. As with virtually every other cottage in Strathquinnan, the door was never locked and Ishbel was soon on her knees at the stove raking out the ash, assembling the kindling, then feeding ever larger logs on to the fire until there was a steady blaze. Stoking it for a last time, she damped it down and returned home in time to make her lads breakfast.

*   *   *   *

Morag McLean was out for the count. The last drops of gin had passed her gullet round about the time her husband was firing rockets at the wreck and she would be in a drunken slumber at least until mid-day.

*   *   *   *

Donald McLeod had phoned David McPhail, the lifeboat secretary, from Oban as soon as he could. The first thing the kindly solicitor did was to hurry to the parish church and tell Anabelle Fraser she could end her vigil. Her two lads were safe and well. More than that, they were heroes. Then he phoned the Rev. Michael Dixon, thinking as he did so that it would do the new man at the manse no harm to meet his flock as a bearer of good tidings when he greeted them at morning worship in less than an hour's time.

Morning worship at Strathquinnan Parish Church was always well attended. However, that Sunday, the only notable absentees were the men of the lifeboat crew. Even Dr Anderson was there in the back pew. There was an atmosphere of relief mingled with a scarcely suppressed joy in the congregation. The praise was sung with even greater enthusiasm than usual and the prayers were fervent expressions of thanksgiving.

Ishbel was there with her two boys. Her personal sense of gratitude was very real, as was her pride in her husband and his crew. However, her feelings were strangely mixed. Somehow she herself seemed so ineffective when compared with Donald. This was not the first time, and, please God, would not be the last time, her husband would save lives at sea. By comparison, anything she had ever done, seemed depressingly mundane. Her thoughts wandered. She glanced across at Mrs Fraser, sitting composedly in the pew she had no doubt occupied all night. Did she know who had lit her fire for her, Ishbel wondered, or had she perhaps been too pre-occupied even to notice it was alight when she went home? Suddenly Ishbel homed in on the Scripture the minister was reading. "Then shall The King say ....'Come...inherit the kingdom....For I was an hungered, and you gave me meat: I was thirsty, and ye gave me drink: I was a stranger, and ye took me in......Inasmuch as ye have done it unto one of the least of these my brethren, ye have done it unto me.'"

The words seemed specially for her that day. Perhaps, after all, the little that she was able to do for the likes of Mrs Fraser, did matter and did not go unnoticed. Somehow, she felt greatly comforted.

Chapter 6

The first representatives of the national press arrived in Strathquinnan on Sunday evening, having hurried up from Glasgow, seemingly oblivious to the fact that motoring into town on the Sabbath day had alienated them not only from all of a Free Church or Free Presbyterian Church persuasion, but also from the majority of the membership of the parish church. With some difficulty they found accommodation, most of them at the Crown Hotel. It would take many free rounds both there and at the Safe Haven, the pub most favoured by the fishing community, before their profaning of the Sabbath would be sufficiently forgiven to loosen tongues. The night sleeper from London brought a further swarm. The dramatic rescue would have been news-worthy at any time, but it had occurred at one of those very rare times when the world was more or less at peace, when there was relative freedom from strife on the industrial front, when the legislation before Parliament was unbelievably boring and, even more strangely, when absolutely no-one in public life had been doing anything scandalous. In other words, the near-tragedy on the Torran Rocks was an absolute God-send for harassed newspaper editors, although perhaps less so than had there been serious loss of life. However, recognising philosophically that they could not expect life to be kind to them all the time and thankful for small mercies, the reporters were there in force.

Both the Crown and the Royal, the only two hotels in Strathquinnan, were packed. Soon, too, were all the guest-houses and bed and breakfast establishments in the neighbourhood. The cost of accommodation rocketed and the lifeboatmen became doubly heroes in every commercial enterprise that could cash in on the boom. Lizzie Stewart, who served behind the bar at week-ends at the Crown, was asked by Angus Wallace, the proprietor, to work full-time for the duration. This was not only because Lizzie had the necessary experience in the licensed trade. Angus Wallace was shrewd enough to realise that, if he leaked to his English clientele that the buxom woman behind the bar was the wife of one of Strathquinnan's heroes, it could only be good for bar sales. So Lizzie found herself the centre of attention, a role in which she excelled herself. However, the story of the rescue was not of enduring interest and, by Wednesday, most of the newspaper reporters were drifting southwards again.

The national scene was unchanged and reporters and editors alike were faced with a distinct dearth of anything that would be guaranteed to sell papers. Timothy Jenkins of the Counties Clarion was determined to milk the Strathquinnan story dry. Apart from his journalistic motivation, he was enjoying his unexpected winter break in the quiet of the Highlands and was in no hurry to go south. After the storm, there was a period of unseasonably bright, warm weather and he could see no good reason to hurry away. Perhaps more compellingly, he fancied his chances with the not-unattractive Lizzie. As the bar closed after lunch that Wednesday afternoon, he suggested to Lizzie, who was about to start her belated lunch-break anyway, that an article about the stress-filled hours of a lifeboatman's wife during the tense periods that the boat was on a mission might not only be of interest to the readers of his rag, but might be so interesting as to attract a considerable fee for the lady in question.

It seemed only reasonable that such an interview should be carried out discreetly, where there was no chance of prying eyes seeing or inquisitive ears listening. That is why Lizzie slipped unobserved into the bedroom occupied by Timothy Jenkins. An hour later, she slipped out again, flushed, sated, and fifty pounds richer. She was unsure whether this represented the usual scale of payment for such a story or whether the fee had perhaps been enhanced by the grateful Timothy, whom she had left lying on the bed looking satisfied to the point of exhaustion as a result of his afternoon's researches on behalf of the Counties Clarion.

Whilst Lizzie's entry into Mr Jenkin's bedroom had however indeed been unobserved, her absence from the public area of the hotel did not go unnoticed. Nor was Timothy Jenkins the only man who fancied his chances with Lizzie Stewart. By intelligent guesswork, Angus Wallace figured out which room she had retired to and was discreetly on hand to watch her exit from it. The hotel proprietor said nothing then, but at closing time that evening, he oiled his way up to Lizzie.

"I think that tomorrow you might like to take a slightly extended lunch-break with me, rather than with Mr Jenkins. He's leaving in the morning anyway, which is perhaps a good thing as I think that your husband would not be best pleased with him if someone told him where you lunched today."

Lizzie blushed crimson. She was not a particularly fastidious young woman, but Wallace was an overweight, middle-aged man with about the same sexual magnetism as a lethargic pig. For a moment she was speechless. Then she rounded on the hotelier.

"Indeed I will not! I gave Mr Jenkins my story and he paid me a fee for it. It was not what you're implying at all!"

"Well, think it over. I'm not sure that your husband would altogether understand why such an interview took so long, nor why it had to be conducted in a bedroom. As to the fee, well, I'm sure he's not the only man who can be generous when he's rightly treated. Off you go now. Think it over and we can talk again in the morning."

Lizzie did think it over. On the whole, she thought it better not to mention the fifty pounds to Alistair. He might not understand. She thought about putting it in her Post Office savings account, but, in a small town where secrets were nearly impossible to keep and gossip was rife, that seemed unwise. She put it in an empty talcum powder box and left it among her other cosmetics. With Alistair snoring gently beside her, she did her thinking long into the night. She did not want to be tied to a small town like Strathquinnan for ever. Perhaps she should try to build up a fund that would enable her to break free some day. If old Wallace wanted her, he could have her, but he would have to pay dearly for the privilege. Her mind made up, she fell asleep.

Chapter 7

'Florence' was in a bad way. The Torran Rocks had torn at her hull and it was only the superb workmanship of her designers and builders that had kept her from total destruction. It was painfully obvious that a major refit was necessary before she could be on station once more. The Royal National Lifeboat Institute sent a relief boat from Cockenzie on the Firth of Forth to Oban. Meanwhile, the yard there had done sufficient repairs for the same passage crew to be able to make a safe return voyage through the Caledonian Canal and down the North Sea to the Lifeboat repair yard on the Forth. This all took time and for over a month there was no lifeboat at all stationed at Strathquinnan, a cause of much distress in a town with a proud lifeboat tradition. The replacement, when it came, was an elderly Watson-class boat, rather smaller and certainly much older than the 'Florence.'

David McPhail began a one-man campaign to get a more modern and larger boat for the town. This led to his visiting Glasgow where he found himself arguing his Branch's case before an imposing committee under the chairmanship of an ex-naval type, one Lt. Commander John Campbell.

Rather pompously, Campbell said, "We do appreciate your concerns, and your care for your crew does you credit. However, you must realise that the resources of the RNLI are limited and we can't give every station a new boat."

"Of course I do understand that, but a lifeboat stationed at Strathquinnan has, at times, to face the open sea in quite horrendous conditions and we owe it to these men to provide the very best. I am not asking for a brand new boat. Something less than ten years old would be better than our old boat or the relief boat that's on station now."

"If the general public shared your views about providing nothing but the best, there would no doubt be more money available. Now, however, we just have to cut our coat to suit our cloth and we can't give you a modern boat just like that."

"I would ask the committee to think again. The 'Florence' could so easily have been overwhelmed in the storm back in January. It's less than fair to send men out in such small craft. Strathquinnan needs a 48-foot boat at least."

"I'm afraid Strathquinnan will have to make do with what we send it. Most of your men are ex-navy and know that there is a centuries-old naval tradition of making the most of the equipment available. You served in the Navy yourself, did you not? You must understand the need to operate under orders. Where was it you served?"

David McPhail had indeed spent six years in the Navy and furthermore had finished the war captain of a light cruiser. This meant he out-ranked the other, but he was not going to say so.

"I was mostly in the Med. Gibraltar, Malta and Alexandria. You're right that the Navy tradition is that we make the most of what we've got, but there's also the tradition that a man fights his ship, sticking to his guns whatever the opposition. I'm no longer at sea but I must fight my personal ship to the best of my ability. I owe it to the lads who take the boat out. And that means pressing as hard as I know how to get the best for Strathquinnan's crew." His apparent arrogance was tempered by the ghost of a smile that flickered over his face as he spoke.

The argument swung to and fro for another hour, but the long-term upshot was that 'Florence' did not return to Strathquinnan. Instead a 54 foot diesel-powered boat built in 1950, the 'Countess', arrived in the town in the autumn of that year, 1958.

Chapter 8

The Rev. Mike Dixon soon settled down among the folk of his new parish. They were a kindly people who, if they had a besetting sin, it was to make promises with no real intention of keeping them. This was not out of disrespect to the minister or the church. Rather, it was a consequence of a misguided kind of respect that meant that they would rather agree to something than risk hurting the minister's feelings by contradicting him. The fact that he might feel justifiably disappointed when they failed to deliver later did not seem to occur to them.

The regard they had for him in his early days was more a matter of a deeply-rooted respect for the church, rather than any esteem they held him in personally. Whatever respect he might one day command in his own right would have to be won. Mike learned to grit his teeth when reference was made to his sainted predecessor. None of the townsfolk seemed to have had too much regard for the man who had been their minister for thirty-four years until the day when the old man spectacularly collapsed and died as he was climbing the pulpit steps. After that he was instantly canonised, even by those who seldom came to hear him in life. Mike lost count of the number of times he heard, "Ah! Mr McAlistair! Now there was a real man of God!"

Dr Kenneth Anderson became a close friend and the younger man learnt much about the town and its people from the wise old doctor. Indeed, Mike was one of a very small, privileged handful in the town who were on first-name terms with their doctor.

"Always remember," the old man counselled, "almost everyone here is related to everybody else. Keep your own thoughts to yourself, unless you want a matter spread throughout the town. If you do want to get something across, just tell it in the strictest confidence to one or two. It's a marvellous local broadcasting system, but it can be devastating if you let slip something you shouldn't. They're a kindly people, by and large, but devilish proud. They never forget an insult or a slight. They'll allow things said and done decades ago to fester in their minds. Feuds can carry on from one generation to another. The men are bad, but the women worse."

Not really so different from his previous parish the other side of Scotland at Arbroath, thought Mike. Perhaps, for all their external differences, the character of the Scottish people was not so widely different as most seemed to suppose as they surveyed east and west, Lowland and Highland, town and country.

The Christian religion divided rather than united the small community, but effectively only on Sundays. The Free Church people went to their church, the Free Presbyterian's to theirs, whilst a majority of the church-going folk went to the parish church, the Church of Scotland. Members of one would not think of attending a service at any of the others. The Free Church despised the Parish Church as decadent and unspiritual, decrying the way it accepted hymns as an equally appropriate expression of worship as the Psalms. Besides which, the Church of Scotland people remained seated at the prayers and stood to sing. Such irreverent conduct was unforgivable to a Free Church mind which instinctively knew that the Almighty was pleased only with Psalms sung by a seated congregation and heard only those prayers offered by people who were standing. The Free Presbyterians despised the Free Church as altogether too liberal in its theology, whilst the Church of Scotland they regarded as a half-way house to the Church of Rome. Meanwhile, every Monday morning fishing boats crewed by representatives of all three churches put to sea and the men worked away happily together, wisely leaving the ecclesiastical differences on shore behind them. Many of these divisions were institutional, rather than personal anyway, the product of dissension and strife in earlier generations and were perpetuated more by tradition than by conviction.

Chapter 9

Lizzie Stewart slipped readily into a new routine at the Crown. With apparent reluctance, she surrendered to her boss's blackmail. He did pay up, not with outstanding generosity, but as the payments were cash from the till with no deductions for tax or national insurance, Lizzie's secret hoard was building up. Most people are good at what they enjoy doing and Lizzie did enjoy sex. She did not like it with Wallace but realised the wisdom of giving good value for money. Through the following weeks, she professed to have agonies of conscience and expressed the desirability of confessing all to her husband. However, her sensitive conscience could be readily anaesthetised by an injection of money into her purse, so the arrangement continued to the sexual gratification of the one and the financial satisfaction of the other.

Angus Wallace had been married to a termagant of a woman who had publicly humiliated him time after time. Many had marvelled at his patience with her and few were surprised when the moody, ill-tempered woman had left her husband and Strathquinnan one night some eleven years ago. The nearly simultaneous departure from the town of a

Canadian airman who had failed to return to his native land at the end of hostilities did not go unnoticed. Since then, Wallace had, to all outward appearances, lived the celibate life appropriate to a single man in the Western Highlands of Scotland. The discreet arrangement with Lizzie Stewart was not Wallace's first romantic liaison, but it was both the longest and, from his perspective, the most satisfying. It was expensive, but, he told himself, much less so and much less of a gamble with happiness than would be the chancy business of remarriage.

How long this arrangement might have continued was anyone's guess, had it not been for Lizzie's growing boldness, her curiosity and her light-fingered willingness to relieve her boss and lover of anything she thought he might not miss. She was very discreet about what she took. Below the bar was the beer-cellar. Adjacent to it were cellars which extended under the other ground-floor rooms. These, as so often happens with such back-waters in the onward flow of a business's development, were stuffed with various items of furniture and bric-a-brac dating back a century and more. Once worthless, some of these memorabilia of times past had now achieved a rarity value as antiques. Ever an enterprising woman, over a period Lizzie turned many of the more portable items into cash. Needless to say, Angus Wallace was blissfully unaware of this small, yet highly profitable business that was going on, literally, under his feet.

The trouble was that the saleable stock was running out. There was a second set of cellars which Wallace kept locked, yet never visited. Lizzie began to wonder what might lie concealed in them. Her opportunity to investigate these came one day when Angus Wallace, with uncharacteristic carelessness, had left his bunch of keys on a shelf under the bar. By good fortune a beer keg ran dry, giving Lizzie the perfect excuse to visit the cellars. Changing the beer keg with exceptional speed, she knew she could afford to spend only two or three minutes investigating the contents of the cellars beyond the closed door. The lock was stiff through lack of use, but she did manage to open the door. Inside were yet more articles of furniture even older than the others. There were several packing cases, trunks and sea-chests, far too many to investigate there and then. Taking only a small risk, Lizzie closed the door, but left it unlocked. When and if Wallace found it open, he would probably assume that he himself had failed to secure it. She ran lightly up the stairs and resumed her position behind the bar, replacing the keys when Wallace's back was turned.

Over the next few weeks, spending only a few minutes at a time in the cellar, Lizzie extracted a number of items which brought a tidy profit. Now that the boom in hotel bookings induced by the press was over, she had returned to her part-time status for most of the week, working only evenings. She did also come in on occasional afternoons as and when her employer desired her to, or, more precisely, desired her body. That left her free to make periodic visits to Oban whenever her brother-in-law, Ewan, was driving his van there to collect meat for his shop. The helpful old pawn-broker in Oban operated his business on a strictly no-questions-asked basis, which was an arrangement that suited

Lizzie well.

After striking a particularly rich seam in the cellar's hidden treasures in that she found a small hat-box containing several really valuable pieces of jewellery, Lizzie began to feel that she had almost exhausted the cellar's potential. There were only two or three cabin trunks left and her earlier experiences with these larger containers was that they were either empty or contained relatively valueless items of

clothing. When a beer keg needed to be changed one Saturday evening, Lizzie sneaked into the cellar and opened a chest that was hard against the back wall. More clothes, musty and unpleasant. She lifted a handful to see if there was anything underneath and found a mummified face gazing up at her. In a flash, she realised that Mrs Wallace had indeed left Strathquinnan eleven years earlier, but not in the way that the town gossips had imagined. Speechless with horror, she dropped the clothes and slammed down the lid. As she swung towards the door, she heard Wallace's voice calling to her as he descended the stairs.

Chapter 10

Lizzie was trapped. Wallace was already at the foot of the steep stair and was faced with, on the one side, the beer-cellar and no sign of his bar-maid and, on the other, the open door to that part of the cellars which he never failed to keep securely locked. Realising her danger, Lizzie ducked down behind the open cellar door and, when Wallace entered, she pushed him firmly in the small of the back, sending him sprawling over the lumber in front of him.

Dashing up the stairs, Lizzie shot past the bar, out the door and ran down the street towards the town square. Panting for breath, she paused and, looking back, saw Wallace rush out of the door of the hotel. Before she could move, he spotted her and started galloping towards her. In near panic, she ran on, trying as she did so to consider her options. She could not go home. Alistair would be out and Wallace would be bound to pursue her there. Al would be with his cronies at the Safe Haven, a strictly male preserve. If she sought refuge there, she would have to do a whole lot more explaining than she had time to rehearse at present. The police house was another possibility, but, on a Saturday night, it was a safe bet that Sergeant Robertson would not be in. Breathless, but well ahead of her overweight and unfit employer, she entered the square. A modest crowd had gathered at a temperance meeting which was in progress. Gratefully, Lizzie skirted round the group and tried to make herself invisible among them.

Throughout the summer months, these occasional temperance meetings were a feature of the local community and were regarded by the righteous, or more accurately, the self-righteous, as an essential part of the on-going battle against the demon drink. The unrighteous did not merely tolerate them; they relished them and especially the opportunity that heckling provided for the demonstration of wit and humour.

That Saturday, the visiting speaker was 'TT' McColl. James McColl was a well-known itinerant ranter against the evils of alcohol. A heavy drinker in his earlier days, he had become a convert to the temperance cause over twenty years earlier, earning the nick-name 'TT' as a result of his crusading zeal as a tee-totaller. Jimmy McColl had had a small farm three or four miles out from Oban. Every Saturday night without fail, he drove his pony and trap into town and drank heavily. When he was full, the bar-staff lifted him back into his trap and slapped the pony's flank. The animal, with a horse-sense that its master at least temporarily lacked, would then trot off to the farm. By the time it had traversed the miles through the cool night air, McColl, though still unsteady on his feet, would usually be in a fit enough state to release the beast from the trap before staggering into bed. Not infrequently, however, he never made it that far and shared the stable all night with the pony.

The turning point in this unspectacular career came one night when the pony was bearing its inebriated and more or less comatose master home. The animal covered the ground at a dignified pace but, as it smelled the smells of home, it accelerated to a gallop for the final furlong. Misjudging the gateway, it all but capsized the trap. The light vehicle heeled over on one wheel and hung at the point of balance for a split second. No doubt it would have gone right over but for the fact that the unconscious Jimmy slid along the seat and fell in the gateway. The trap bounced down on both wheels again and the pony proceeded home, quite oblivious to the fact that its master was now lying in a crumpled heap at the road-side.

In those far off, pre-war days, traffic was very light on all country roads, especially at that time of night. Jimmy McColl therefore might well have spent the night where he lay. However, there had been a funeral in Benderloch and Alf Cattanach, the undertaker, and his brother-in-law and assistant, Willie Miller, were homeward-bound after the prolonged obsequies at which they, too, had drunk perhaps more than was wise. The elderly Rolls-Royce hearse steamed silently through the night on a slightly meandering course, with Alf Cattanach at the helm. As it approached McColl's farm, the vehicle's watery headlights picked out the farmer's recumbent form. Cattanach pushed the gear lever into neutral and applied the brakes. His large craft gradually lost way and came to a halt beside the still-unconscious man. With the slow and solemn movements which alcohol inspires in some, the two undertakers dismally assessed the situation. McColl was bleeding mildly from a graze to his forehead. Whether his lack of consciousness was due to drink or concussion was hard to say. The two good Samaritans were perhaps inclined to diagnose the former as they bent over the unconscious man and received the full effect of the alcoholic fumes.

A very serious debate then ensued. Should they take the farmer home and dump him in his bed to sleep it off? Should they seek medical help? On balance, taking him with them to Oban and the hospital there seemed to be the wisest course. However, there was a snag. There were but two seats in the hearse. At this stage in the day's funereal activities, there would normally have been adequate space in the back for one, so long as he did not wish to sit upright. However, Cattanach had taken the opportunity to bring back with him a new coffin that the joiner at North Connel had been making for him. There was no room for both McColl and a coffin.

The undertakers gravely considered their options. In the sepulchral tones appropriate to their chosen profession, they debated the problem at some length. Eventually, a conclusion was reached. They would leave the coffin discreetly at the road-side and return for it the next morning. This would leave room in the back of the hearse for the horizontal passenger. Meanwhile, a groggy Jimmy McColl was on the threshold of consciousness. He slowly took in the fact that he was prostrate beside the road. He became aware of the presence of a large vehicle whose side-lights were now the only source of illumination. He took in the classic lines of the lordly radiator, then the unmistakable body-shape of the hearse. As his mind became marginally clearer, he saw behind it the two, sad, black-clad undertakers wearing tall, top hats unloading a coffin and laying it down beside him. Sobriety returned in an instant.

"No! No! No! I'm alive! I'm alive!," he exclaimed repeatedly. And ever after, at least, according to legend, he never touched a drop.

Chapter 11

Lizzie looked anxiously around her. Suddenly, she spotted Wallace's perspiring face diagonally opposite her in the small crowd. Their eyes met for a fraction of a second, then Lizzie ducked and edged backwards into a narrow pend. Once again, she took to her heels. Wallace lost vital seconds trying to ease his way through the crowd without drawing too much attention to himself. He reached the far end of the pend, but there was no sign of Lizzie. Baffled, he returned to the Crown.

Lizzie had stopped running. In a doorway opposite the chip shop, she paused for breath. If Wallace appeared, she could dash into the shop, secure in the knowledge that he would do nothing in front of a crowd. She went over her options. She could tell Al. She could tell the police. She could send an anonymous letter to the police. All these scenarios had the positive arguments of securing her from any attempt on Wallace's part to silence her. The down side was that she would have to explain what she was doing, poking around in the cellar. She might just manage to conceal her virtual prostitution but she could hardly expect to emerge without being branded as a thief. Mentally, she added up the contents of the talcum powder box. About £475, more than her husband would earn in a year, but scarcely enough for her to take and disappear to Glasgow or London with. Besides, there would be no transport out of Strathquinnan until Monday now.

Suddenly, she arrived at a decision. She marched boldly up the street and strode into the Crown where Angus Wallace was struggling to serve the evening's customers. Without a word, she took her place beside him at the bar and began serving as though nothing had happened. At length there was a lull in the demand for drinks. Wallace was beside her.

"Lizzie," he said in a whisper, "I know what you're thinking, but you're wrong. It's not what you think. I didn't kill her. Goodness knows, I had more than enough reason to, but I didn't. We had had an argument after hours. I had been carrying empty barrels up from the cellar and had just reached the top when she struck out at me. I stumbled and pushed her away. The next thing I knew was that she had tripped down the stairs and was lying in a heap at the bottom. At the very least, I was facing a very long sentence for manslaughter. More likely, it would have been a hanging matter. I hid her in that chest and you know the rest."

"Aye," replied Lizzie, "and so will my husband if I am not safely home before he is. I've told him the whole story in a letter and left it where you won't find it but where he will if I'm not home tonight. I'm not coming back here after tonight, but it's going to take quite a lot to help me forget what I saw."

Wallace could take a hint. As a customer came to the

bar for a drink, he gestured to Lizzie to serve him. Then he himself slipped into the office and opened the safe. At the next lull in custom, he slid a sealed envelope into Lizzie's hand.

"There's a hundred quid in there. That's all I've got. Come back on Monday and we'll talk about the future."

Lizzie would have loved to have told him that there was no way she was going to risk meeting him again, but her natural greed got the better of her. She nodded her assent and, ten minutes before closing time, she abruptly left.

Chapter 12

Two people in Strathquinnan scarcely slept a wink that night. Lizzie was torn between the twin prospects of, on the one hand, riches to come if she could lean hard enough on Angus Wallace and, on the other, of having always to look over her shoulder in case he decided that the risk of killing her was worth taking.

Angus Wallace was in a quandary. He knew instinctively that, whatever he gave Lizzie, she would be back for more. That was the norm with blackmailers and Lizzie had all the hallmarks of a rapacious one. She was none too bright, but he believed her story about leaving a message for Al as an insurance against anything happening to her. He had either to silence her, or be bled white for ever more. Eventually he decided she would have to go and in circumstances in which any letter would perish with her.

Sunday passed uneventfully. Lizzie made sure that she was never alone and, by evening, was managing to feel relaxed. At bed-time, the sleeplessness of the night before was catching up with her and she snuggled up to Al. The pair soon drifted off to sleep. An hour or more later, Al sat up suddenly, wakening his wife as he did so.

"What's up?" she demanded.

"Shush! I think I heard someone out the back."

The two listened in a tense silence. A very slight, furtive noise came from somewhere beyond the back door. Al leapt out of bed and hauled on his trousers. He might have reached the back-door silently had he not tripped noisily over his boots. Delayed only for a second, he was still too late to see anyone as he peered out into the darkness.

"That's funny," he remarked, pulling on his boots. "I'm sure there was someone out there. I'm going to have a better look."

He grabbed a torch and went out into the yard behind the house. The Stewart's cottage was one of a terrace of seven, each with a postage-stamp size front garden and a much larger yard at the back. Access to this yard for a mid-terrace cottage like Al's was either through the house from the front door or by way of an alley at the rear which ran the length of the seven cottages. Al leant over the gate of this and flashed his torch to left and right along the alley. There was nothing to see. He turned back to the house. Then his torch picked out a one gallon oil-can. Knowing it was not his, Al picked it up, opened it and sniffed. Petrol! Now how did that come to be there?

He put the can in the small shed along with lobster-pots, old nets and other fishing gear. Back in the cottage, he discussed the mystery with his wife.

"Now, who would leave a gallon of petrol out there? No-one here has a car, but there are a couple of motor-bikes and a few out-boards. Someone might want petrol, but why abandon it in our yard?"

Lizzie paled. She immediately knew where the petrol had come from and what the bearer of it had intended. For a moment she was about to tell her husband everything. Then her greed overcame her fear.

"Could someone have been stealing it? You know, siphoning it out of a car in the Royal Hotel's car-park. They might have been disturbed and ran down this way, dumping the evidence in case they got caught."

"Possible, I suppose," said her husband slowly. "Who the devil would it be, though? And why our yard?"

Eventually, Al drifted off to sleep, but Lizzie was awake all night.

Chapter 13

Back at the Crown, Angus Wallace was sweating. He had had a narrow shave outside the Stewart's cottage. He was confident that he had not been seen, but he was no nearer solving his problem. The hotel was in darkness. There were only three guests and they had retired to bed hours ago. Sitting down in the dark bar, Wallace poured himself what might be fairly described as a double, double whisky. Under its mellowing influence, he became calmer. Suddenly light dawned on his troubled mind. He would do what he should have done years ago. He would take the sea-chest and its hideous contents and drop them in the quarry pond ten miles up the Strontian road. Then he could call that greedy vixen's bluff!

He slipped out the back door and reversed his Wolseley as close to it as he could. Then, fortified with another whisky, he descended the cellar stairs. Along the side of the stair-case was a long thick plank standing on its edge. Whenever there was a delivery of beer, this plank was put face down on the stairs so as to provide a smooth surface to slide the barrels down. Wallace now positioned it so that he could shove the sea-chest up it. It was hard enough work clearing a passage through the accumulation of furniture and junk to enable him to pull the chest to the foot of the stairs. Once there, he took a breather and found a length of rope. He then tied the chest securely shut and formed some loops to give some hand-holds. At first he tried pulling the chest up, but without success. He rested once more and then lifted one end of the chest on to the plank. With great difficulty, he positioned himself behind it and began to push. Inch by inch the heavy chest went up the gradient. Towards the top Wallace was feeling the strain. The sweat was lashing off him. He was puffing like a steam engine. A constricting force like tightening steel bands gripped his chest. Everything went red. Then it went black. Wallace slid back down the stairs with the accelerating weight of the chest behind him. When he fetched up on the floor below, the chest fell right across his prostrate form. So Angus Wallace perished under the weight of his unlamented wife.

When his cold and stiff body was found the next day, there was general sympathy, mixed with perplexity. No-one could think why the hotelier had not waited for help if he wanted to move such a heavy chest. As it did not seem very relevant to the police inquiry into the circumstances of his death, no-one bothered to open the chest. So it was that, several weeks later, a very surprised distant cousin who had been amazed to discover that he had fallen heir to a country hotel, made a discovery that literally would haunt him to the end of his days. Lizzie, however, was made of sterner stuff and, all danger past, was now sleeping the sleep of the innocent.

Chapter 14

After the drama on the Torran Rocks, the months that followed were humdrum for the lifeboat crew. They were called out several times over the summer, usually because of the stupidity of city-folk on holiday. There was the family cut off by the rising tide, a potentially disastrous situation had not the alarm been raised in good time, but, in the event, a routine rescue on a perfect summer's day. There were several yachts in trouble, often because of badly-maintained engines or inadequate equipment. More often, however, the situation was made worse by the inexperience or reckless stupidity of the amateurs crewing such boats.

As summer gave way to autumn, the new boat, the 'Countess', was put through her paces. In a series of exercises in varying weather conditions, the crew got to know and respect their new craft. However, it was not until the equinoctial gales of late autumn that she really had her baptism of fire, if such an inappropriate expression could be used of thirty hours when the boat seemed to be more under the water than on top of it.

The drama began, as so often before, with the crash of the maroons detonating high above the roof-tops of

Strathquinnan. It was just after midnight on a wild night, although, as the wind unusually was blowing from the north-east, the town was sheltered from the worst of the blast by the circle of hills behind it. The predictable scramble followed for a place on the crew. The new boat, too large for the boat-house, was moored to a special pontoon in the harbour so there was none of the drama of the slip-way launch that had been so heart-stirring when 'Florence' put to sea. Indeed, there was almost a sense of anti-climax as the moorings were slipped and, with a muffled rumble from her twin diesels, 'Countess' nosed her way out of the harbour. The seas were deceptively calm in the shelter of the land and, even after the boat had rounded Eilean Sgreadan, the following wind raised only a moderate swell. However, as the land fell farther and farther behind, it became evident that the night ahead was going to be exciting.

* * * *

As the 'Countess' made her way out to the open sea, the crowd at the boat-house dispersed. Irene McGregor settled down in bed with her book. Morag dug out her gin bottle. Anabelle Fraser made her way to her pew in the parish church. And Ewan Stewart took his sister-in-law to her home to provide the comfort Lizzie craved.

* * * *

A Liberian tanker had lost all power and was drifting

helplessly in the Sea of the Hebrides at the southern approaches to the Minches. The area she was in was studded with islets, some big enough to sustain a small croft, many mere rocks with sparse and patchy vegetation. Radio contact was quickly established and the coxswain was soon speaking to the first-mate of the stricken vessel, apparently one of very few on board who spoke any English.

The wind was now force eight, hitting their port quarter and making 'Countess' skew as she fought to maintain a straight course. Visibility was poor, worsening by the minute as the wind whipped the crest off each wave and showered it across the lifeboat. There was also heavy cloud and occasional squalls of rain, all of which added to the problems facing the lifeboat crew. Whilst McLeod knew fairly accurately his own position, the tanker was only able to give them a very approximate fix. The driving rain soaked their backs as they ran before the wind. Heavy waves crashed against the lifeboat. Visibility was soon nearly negligible, but every man watched with eyes peeled for any sign of the ship. At last, far out into the Hebridean Sea, McLeod reckoned that they were now dangerously near the southern isles of the Outer Hebrides and the thought of having these islands and reefs down-wind of the lifeboat frankly terrified him. He swung the 'Countess' southwards and held a steady course for a couple of miles before turning east into the teeth of the wind.

The problem was that the tanker's master had only a hazy idea of his present position. The ship had been drifting for several hours at the whim of wind and tide and placing his vessel to within three miles was impossible. With visibility down to a quarter of a mile as rain-squalls eased and substantially less for most of the time, this made finding her difficult in the extreme. Trying to bring the lifeboat close to the tanker would be nearly impossible even if they were lucky enough to locate her. The 'Countess' ploughed eastward into the gale which was by now force nine gusting force ten at times. Every five minutes, the crew fired a rocket, hoping the tanker's crew might spot it. For two hours, making barely five knots into the wind, the lifeboat held its course. The two craft remained in constant radio contact, but, as the first streaks of dawn lightened the charcoal-grey clouds in the north-east, they still were lost to each other.

Dawn brought no let-up in the weather. If anything, both the wind and the waves were rising. Only when the lifeboat was momentarily on the crest of a wave was there any real chance of seeing anything. Even then, the rain and spray cut visibility down to a matter of yards. When the boat was in a trough, all that could be seen was the twin walls of water ahead and astern. The cloud level now was too low to hope for any help from aircraft. As the weather worsened, McLeod began to wonder if he dare try to put about. So long as the bows were plunging into the wind and the waves, the boat was fairly safe. To the east, the nearest land was at least twenty miles away, or four hours at their present speed. As he neared the coast, he could expect the waves to moderate, so putting about there should not be too hazardous. Where the tanker was, he had no idea. Indeed, deep down inside, the coxswain was increasingly feeling the burden of responsibility for his own crew's safety even though he longed to be able to rescue the tanker's crew.

Chapter 15

David McPhail was a worried man. He should have been at his office, but there was no way he could concentrate on his legal business while seven lifeboatmen were pitting their lives against the Atlantic. He had sat huddled over a radio-set throughout the night, monitoring the conversations between the tanker, the coastguards and the lifeboat. Now he was picking up more static than conversation. The calls from the tanker were controlled, but an underlying urgency was increasingly giving way to something like desperation.

Then, just after eleven, came a disjointed message from the tanker. She had struck a reef. The lifeboat replied and the coastguard, aided by the Royal Navy, were at last successful in getting a fix on the position of both vessels. The lifeboat was thirteen miles south south-east of the tanker. The wind in the vicinity was force ten, gusting force eleven at times, with the meteorology office forecasting no let-up until evening. It was all too obvious that the stricken tanker would have broken up long before then.

· · · · · · · · · · · ·

On the 'Countess', Donald McLeod listened to the plea from the doomed tanker as she struck the reef. He got the fix on its and on his own position from Oban coastguards. The ship was at least two hours sailing in these conditions. Would the wreck stay afloat long enough for the lifeboat to do any good? Dare he try to put about in these mountainous seas? Even if he made it in time to the wreck, could the lifeboat hold station long enough to take anyone off? Holding her bows into the wind, he shouted his thoughts and his fears to his fellows. To a man, they urged him to turn. They could not return to a safe haven without even trying. Whilst McLeod was still pondering what to do, the wind seemed to moderate somewhat. He nodded to McLean who hurriedly radioed that they were putting about.

With a shout to his crew to hold on, McLeod pushed the throttles wide open and swung the wheel to starboard. With a sickening lurch, the bows came round and the craft corkscrewed as it slid down the back of a roller. Then, just as the boat lay broadside to the waves, a gigantic wall of water smashed into and on to them. The boat heeled right over and, for few seconds, the propellers screamed above the men before the racing engines cut. For what seemed an eternity, the craft was completely upside down. Then, miraculously, another huge wave rolled her back on to her keel once more.

. . . .

McPhail was sweating as he heard McLean say that the 'Countess' was putting about and would make her best speed to the scene of the wreck. For long, tense minutes he waited, but no further word came from the lifeboat. Either her radio had packed up or she had been overwhelmed as she came round broadside on to the waves.

The next few hours were a living nightmare. The messages from the tanker told of the ship's back breaking just forward of the bridge and of the whole forward section being dashed to pieces on the rocks. The crew were now huddled on the stern. All electric power had failed, leaving the radio operating ever more weakly on battery power alone. Then, about two in the afternoon, came a last, desperate plea for help, followed by a few disjointed sentences which were so faint as to be unintelligible. Then there was only silence. David McPhail sat with his head in his hands and wept.

Chapter 16

Early in the morning, Mike Dixon had slipped into the church, disregarding the doctor's advice earlier in the year. He nodded gravely to the silent Mrs Fraser and sat down in one of the pews. He was a man to whom prayer was real and vital, but that morning he prayed as he had never prayed before, his head in his hands and with tears trickling through his fingers. He knew each man on that boat. He knew their families. He knew at least something of their lives and loves, their hopes and dreams. So he 'wept and felt and prayed for all'.

At lunch-time, somewhat more composed, the minister left the church. The rain was still falling in torrents and the wind, blowing now harder than ever from the east over the town, eddied and swirled through the streets. David McPhail had not been alone in following events on his radio and here and there in the town were anxious faces as friends and relatives alike waited for news. The tanker was still on air, but nearly two hours had elapsed since the last message from the 'Countess'. Small groups huddled wherever there was shelter, exchanging the scanty bits of news they had been able to glean and speculating, sometimes hopeful, often despairing, about the fate of their lifeboat crew.

. . . .

The coxswain looked anxiously round. One, two, three, four, five, six! They were all still aboard! Two or three already had blood streaming down their wet faces, having obviously taken a battering as the boat capsized. All looked very shaken.

Tam Ross began to try to restart the engines. The starboard one caught, running very roughly. The port one coughed repeatedly, but that was all. Dod McLean tried the radio, but after a few minutes he shook his head. Cautiously, the mechanic slipped the starboard engine into gear and eased open the throttle. The engine coughed. It spluttered. Then it died. All repeated efforts were to no avail. Neither engine was going to start.

"Sorry, Skip! I think there must be dirt or water in the fuel and being up-ended has shaken it all over the place. When the sea moderates, I'll no doubt get them going, but it'll be well-nigh impossible in this swell."

"OK! We'd better get out a sea-anchor and prepare to ride it out. There's no point in running down the batteries if the engines are not going to start. The morning forecast was that the wind will moderate by night-fall. Perhaps you can do something then," yelled McLeod in reply.

What he did not say was that that kind of time-scale was hours too late for the Liberian tanker's crew. The men of Strathquinnan had tried. They had done their utmost. But they had failed.

The hours that followed took on a nightmarish quality. Thousands of gallons of freezing water pounded down on the boat. The seven men secured themselves with life-lines and huddled in the cockpit. Three or four times, the 'Countess' was hit by exceptional waves, but, riding at her sea-anchor and no longer broadside on to the waves, she rolled alarmingly, but stayed upright. As the afternoon wore on, the wind did slacken almost imperceptibly. The howl round the mast and the cockpit coaming lessened and, twice in the early evening, the men heard the roar of multiple aero engines high above the clouds. Were the airmen looking for them? Were they hunting for the tanker? Surely the presence of the planes was not coincidental and it was immensely comforting to think that they were not totally alone.

Having no radio was a terrible loss. Each man knew that the absence of word from the 'Countess'' would mean hours of agony in Strathquinnan. What they did not know was that they were being spared the anguish of listening helplessly to the last messages from the stricken tanker.

. . . .

Mike Dixon returned to the church carrying a bag containing sandwiches and a thermos flask. With great difficulty he managed to persuade Anabelle Fraser to drink some tea, but all his cajoling would not induce her to eat so much as a biscuit. Soon after two, David McPhail slipped into a pew at the back, his kindly face grey with strain and sorrow.

Then, one by one, more of the townsfolk came, each sitting in a silence broken only by the occasional muted sob.

So the afternoon wore on. The rain fell unceasingly. Just before six, McPhail slipped out in time to catch the shipping forecast. The usual litany of sea-areas round the east, the south and, at last, the west of the British Isles droned past his unhearing ears until he heard 'Malin: Severe gale nine, moderating to force five by 1900 hours. Visibility poor.'

Force five by 7pm! There would still be some daylight then. Quickly, he telephoned the coast-guard at Oban.

"Aye! It sounds promising, but visibility's still impossible. The RAF sent up a couple of Shackletons, but, with a cloud ceiling of less than 200 feet, they were unable to see anything. They're flying hourly sorties. I'll phone if we get anything."

McPhail sat anxiously by his telephone, rising every so often to look out the window. The weather was indeed moderating. Towards six, the rain stopped and the clouds started to lift. Just before seven, the phone rang.

"Great news! Your boat's still afloat and there are definitely survivors, although the Shackleton's crew couldn't get a count. The 'Countess' is dead in the water, riding at sea-anchor. Oban and Mallaig boats are both on their way. Their ETA'll be about 11pm. Unfortunately, there's still too much wind for a helicopter and the light will have failed before the wind moderates enough for one to take off. I'll keep you posted."

Almost too choked to reply, McPhail spluttered his

thanks. He put down the phone and gave way to a burst of tears. A deeply emotional man, he fought to regain his composure, knowing he had news that the crowd agonising in St Columba's must hear.

He stumbled up the knoll to the church, peered round inside until he saw Dixon. Sliding into the pew beside the minister, he hastily whispered the news. Immediately, Mike dashed to the front.

"The boat's still afloat. An RAF plane has seen them and there definitely are survivors. We'll have to wait some hours for more accurate news, but Mallaig and Oban have sent their lifeboats. Keep praying, but let your prayers be mingled with thanks!"

An audible sigh of relief swept through the church. The news was good, although there might yet prove to have been some casualties. So the waiting continued.

. . . .

As the day wore on, the cloud level above the 'Countess' began to lift. A rumble in the sky far to the north roused the lifeboatmen. The evening light flashed on the fuselage and wings of a large plane several miles away, flying east to west. Quickly they fired off two red flares in quick succession. The plane swung round and headed directly towards them. At less than a couple of hundred feet it roared over the helpless 'Countess'. Then it banked steeply and came even lower. The airmen in the cockpit were clearly visible and the Strathquinnan men waved enthusiastically.

The giant plane climbed higher and started a circling manoeuvre high above the boat. Ten minutes later, at an incredibly slow speed for such a big machine, it made a low pass and, as it did so, an Aldis light began to blink.

"Oban and Mallaig lifeboats coming. ETA 1100 hours. Forecast good."

Immensely comforted, the tired men settled down to wait. Tam was fretting. He would have liked to have tried restarting the engines. However, there was no point in doing so now, except that his pride was hurt. The engines had raced as the propellers had lifted out of the water and had, at least for a few seconds, been running upside down. What that might have done to the bearings as the oil-pumps circulating the lubricating oil vainly pumped air, he had no way of telling. At all events, it would be better now to submit to the humiliation of a tow, rather than take unnecessary risks that might ruin the expensive engines.

The hours crawled by. The wind did fall away towards evening and the ocean settled down to a long, deep swell. Almost on the dot of eleven o'clock, the mast-light of the Mallaig boat could be seen in the north, its cox being guided in by the Shackleton that still droned incessantly overhead, dropping flares at regular intervals. Half an hour later, the Oban boat arrived. A loud-hailer conference followed. The first priority was a radio message for Strathquinnan. "No casualties!"

Then it was agreed that five of the Strathquinnan men should transfer to the Mallaig boat, their places being taken by two men from each of the other lifeboats. The 'Countess' would then be towed to Oban, escorted to calm waters by the Mallaig boat. Once the crippled boat was judged to be safe, the Mallaig lifeboat would then return to its base, after dropping the five 'Countess' men off at Strathquinnan on the way.

Everything went to plan. McLeod and Tam Ross

stayed on the 'Countess' and, for the second time that year, the coxswain left his command at Oban and went home by bus!

Chapter 17

Donald McLeod celebrated his 40th birthday just before Christmas. It was a simple, family occasion, but, for Donald, a time for reflection. He had packed more than most into his adult years. Thinking back, he remembered his 20th birthday, way back in 1938. Already, the clouds of war were gathering for those who had eyes to see them. Perhaps that was why Mary and John McLeod had made such a special occasion of his 20th, instead of waiting for his 21st. His 21st had been spent on the bridge of a pitching freighter somewhere south of Iceland, his nerves strained and his eyes peeled as he scoured the Atlantic waves for the tale-tale sign of a U-boat's periscope. That trip had been uneventful, but, before peace returned nearly six years later, he had had two ships sunk under him and had lost many good companions to the cold, cruel waters of the Atlantic and Arctic Oceans.

Looking back, Donald realised that the war years had had a hardening effect on him and he realised that he did not really like the kind of man he had become by the time hostilities ended. What he might eventually have become, he did not dare think. The loss of so many friends had made him detached and rather slow to risk any close ties with anyone.

He had been hurt too much and too many times to risk readily suffering more. A hard, protective shell developed round him which might have progressively blighted his life, were it not for Ishbel.

Ishbel was not a Strathquinnan lass. Her folk were from the Isle of Lewis. When her mother died and her father had had to come to hospital at Oban, Ishbel had moved there. Donald was 28 when they met and 30 when they were married. Slowly, Ishbel's gentle influence had broken down at least some of the emotional armour with which Donald had protected himself. The coming of his boys, David, now a tubby eight-year-old, then Robert, a couple of year's younger, had completed the mellowing effect and enabled him to push the horrific memories of the War into the dark recesses of his mind.

For all that Ishbel had drawn Donald out of his shell, he was still a man happy with his own company and therefore more than content with his lonely work fishing for lobsters. For the most part, it was a comfortable way of earning a living. Like every kind of fishing, there were good times and bad times. However, it did mean he did not voyage far from home and each night he curled up beside Ishbel in their own bed. The winter months were tough. It was cold and uncomfortable work locating each lobster-pot, hauling up the ropes, sodden with nearly ice-cold water, then setting the now empty pots ready for another catch. Only during the worst winter storms, did Donald stay ashore. Otherwise, he was out every day, sometimes in brilliant winter sunshine, more often in rain or sleet.

The winter gave way to spring and, early in April, Donald was out in his boat. 'Helen' was an old wooden boat, sixteen feet long and powered by a noisy but reliable Seagull outboard engine. One day he would get a better boat. 'Helen' was showing her age. She was rotting away slowly and Donald realised that he would be lucky to get more than another year out of her. However, she would have to do for now.

Donald steered 'Helen' out of Strathquinnan just after nine in the morning. He skirted round Eilean Sgreadan and chugged along to the first of the rocky islets off which his lobster-pots were set. The morning was reasonably successful and, by the time he took a break soon after noon, he had quite a satisfactory catch. Lunch over, he re-started the engine and headed farther out to Eilean Dubh. Fishing off the west side of Eilean Dubh was an experiment. Off the island, there was a long, low reef much of which barely broke the surface at low tide and Donald felt it worth the gamble to spend some time laying pots there. It was considerably farther from Strathquinnan than his usual grounds but, as these were showing signs of being over-fished, he was keen to find new, productive fishing grounds.

The run out to Eilean Dubh took nearly an hour and then a further fifteen minutes elapsed as he skirted round the north side of the island to where he had left his pots on the western side. As the low-lying island slipped by to port, Donald looked at its bare, rocky shore-line, with the sparse vegetation above it and wondered how anyone had ever managed to eke out an existence on it. Yet, until the out-break of war in 1939, it had been home to an old couple who lived in the little croft that he could just see nestling close to the shore at the western end of the two-mile long narrow island. The army had had an observation post on it, but, since the war ended, Eilean Dubh had lain deserted, visited only occasionally in the summer months by groups of anglers from Glasgow. These camped out on the island and Donald had often seen their camp-fires flickering in the summer twilight. Now, in April, it looked cold and desolate.

Perhaps because he was distracted by the island and all these memories, Donald failed to notice a great spar of waterlogged wood the size of a telegraph pole. It had probably been part of the deck cargo of some freighter and had been washed overboard in a winter storm. Now, almost totally submerged, it lay dead ahead of 'Helen'. Donald looked up just in time to see the end of the spar break the surface before it disappeared under 'Helen's' bow. Donald thrust the tiller over but the little boat's head had barely begun to swing when the spar crashed through the none-too-sound bow planks, skewering poor 'Helen'. The wood penetrated six feet or more. Then the forward motion of the boat made it swing round tearing a huge gash in the side. 'Helen's nose went down and, with the Seagull still driving her forwards, the sea gushed in.

Donald threw himself overboard on to the plank that had done the damage. Like almost every fisherman in Strathquinnan and certainly like the entire life-boat crew, he could not swim a stroke. By the time he recovered himself, clinging as best he could to the weed-covered plank, 'Helen' had gone. One or two fragments remained floating around, but that was all. Being on the water was natural to Donald. Being in it was not. He had been warmly clad and it took several seconds for the icy water to penetrate his clothes but, as it did, he realised he would last only an hour or so before exposure and cold finished him off.

Donald pulled himself up on the plank. With his eye-level so close to the water, his horizon was severely limited. However, he could see the shore of the island a couple of hundred yards off. Wrapping his arms round the plank, he began to kick his legs. The wood was so saturated and its weight so great that he began to wonder if he was making any headway at all. Furthermore, although there was a negligible wind, the tide might well carry him past the island. Inch by inch, man and plank moved towards the shore. Latterly, it was his will-power alone that was forcing his numb legs to kick. At length, Donald paused for breath, all but exhausted. As his feet trailed below him, they struck solid ground. Stumbling, now chest-deep in water and still leaning heavily on the plank, he made his way shore-ward. At last, he pulled himself out on to solid ground. Collapsing on the sand, he hauled huge breaths into his aching lungs. The first part of his battle for survival was over, but he was far from being safe. The light breeze whipped round him, chilling him further. He tried to stand, but his legs were like jelly. Numb to above the knees, his limbs would not obey him. He flopped on the sand once again, utterly exhausted. A not-unpleasant stupor began to creep over him. He could do with a sleep. Just as he was in fact dozing off, some survival instinct deep within him shouted to him that, if he did sleep, he would never wake up. The will to live was vital. Donald had seen men lose it when, their ship torpedoed, twenty-three men had huddled in a ship's boat. Some took their turn at bailing and forced their unwilling bodies to go on. Others had sunk into lethargy, despair and death.

Forcing himself back into consciousness, Donald started to crawl. He might not be able to stand, but he could crawl. He reckoned he knew the direction to take to reach the deserted croft. What he would find in that hovel, he did not know, but he did know that he must get out of the wind or it would sap away whatever strength he still had. Crawling is an ungainly and inefficient way of getting about. It does, however, require great effort and the expenditure of that effort generates heat. Forcing himself onwards, Donald began to mutter, "I must not give up! I must not give up!"

At the top of a small crest, he paused and rested. There was no danger of him falling asleep now. The terrible pain of the circulation coming back into his lower limbs ensured that. He was nearer the croft than he thought. With a struggle, he scrambled on to his feet and staggered the remaining yards to the cottage. The rotting door swung on rusty hinges. Inside was dark and dank. Donald's eyes slowly became accustomed to the gloom. There was just the one room. Obviously all smaller items of furniture had been removed when the building was abandoned, but an old table under the one window remained. In a bed-recess was a double bed with a rotting mattress still in place on it. The window, though nearly opaque with the accumulation of salt-spray outside and cob-webs inside, was intact and a rag of curtain still hung over it.

Although the inside temperature was no doubt very much the same as that outside, there was an illusion of warmth as Donald came into the shelter of the croft and the breeze no longer chilled his body. The anglers had gathered half a dozen fish boxes and had piled them three-high on either side of the table to serve as chairs. The only other evidence that anglers had been squatting there were a number of empty beer-bottles.

Donald looked round the wretched room with despair flooding through him when, on the mantle-piece above the open fire he saw a couple of candles, each about an inch long, stuck in the necks of empty bottles. More importantly, in a jam-jar, was a box of matches. The lid was securely screwed down. The matches might just be dry, in which case he would live. Or they might be damp, in which case he would almost certainly die.

His hands still numb with cold, Donald tried to open the lid, but it would not budge. The jar slipped through his clumsy fingers and shattered as it struck the hearth. He reached down and picked up the match-box. He opened it. About twenty matches were left. With great difficulty, he extracted one and struck it on the box. It spluttered and smoked, but did not light. A wave of despair swept over him. Carefully, he pulled one of the candles out of its bottle and laid it on its side on the mantle-piece with the wick overhanging the front. Then he drew out six matches. Holding them bunched together, he rubbed them hard on the box. They sputtered, smoked then, briefly, flared. His hands wobbling, he held them under the protruding wick. The candle spluttered into life and an immense wave of relief surged through Donald. He would live! He knew it!

Carefully, he lit the other candle and carried it over to the far corner. Round it he positioned two of the fish-boxes, arguing to himself that, if a freak draught put out one candle, the other might survive. That done he set about stamping on one of the fish-boxes until he had reduced it to match-wood. He then broke some of the smaller pieces down even further and built a small pyramid of splinters in the fire-place. He was now ready to light the fire, but before he did so, he knew he must accumulate sufficient fuel to sustain the fire all night. The fish-boxes were dry and would burn well but would soon burn themselves out. The table was too substantial for him to break up without any kind of tool. The bed-fame, too, was of a heavy construction and would not be much help.

Somewhat unwillingly, Donald went outside. In the adjacent barn he found a bundle of rotten fence-posts. These he could put end-on into the fire, progressively feeding them in as they burnt. They would help, but he needed still more. There was nothing for it but to go and forage along the tide-line for drift-wood. He had perhaps an hour and a half of daylight left. He must use it well if he were to survive the night.

Before going to the beach, he returned to the cottage dragging the fence-posts with him. Carefully, he lifted the stubby candle down and poked it into the pyramid of splinters. The dry wood caught quickly and soon he was feeding, first the larger pieces of fish-box, then the fence-posts into it. The heat worked wonders for his morale.

It was with an effort of will that he went out into the chill evening air and started to forage for fuel. After six trips along the shore, he felt he had enough. Some of it was fairly wet, but there was a good heart in the fire and he positioned the fuel round it so that it would dry out at least somewhat. As the temperature began to build up in the small room, so did a fetid mixture of odours. The remaining fish-boxes made their peculiar contribution, as did the rotten mattress. The floor

nearest the fire started to steam. The damp plaster on the walls had an aroma all of its own. The window steamed up.

Donald tipped the table on its side about five feet back from the fire, its top facing the blaze. Then he stripped off, wringing out each sodden garment as he did so. He hung his clothes over the table-top, positioned a fish-box in front of it and, stark naked, sat down gingerly on the rough wood. He leant back on the table-top which was reflecting the heat back towards the fire, closed his eyes and soaked in the warmth. The fire blazed on. The temperature rose and with it, both the humidity and the stench. The wretched hovel would have turned any normal person's stomach. To Donald, glad to feel almost too warm, it was a little corner of heaven.

Chapter 18

Donald would usually be home by four. By five, Ishbel was
sufficiently worried to be down at the harbour quizzing the
other fishermen. By six, with less than two hours daylight
left, she sought out David McPhail. Ten minutes later the
maroons soared skywards and soon the 'Countess' was at
sea. The big problem for Dod McLean, coxswain in the
absence of Donald McLeod, was that they had only the
haziest idea where to search. They knew Donald's traditional
fishing-grounds, but they also knew that he had been
researching alternative sites for his lobster-pots.
Furthermore, as was to be expected of any fisherman in a
competitive situation, Donald played his cards very close to
his chest. No-one knew where, among the various islands and
reefs that dotted the area, he might have been fishing. In
failing light, the life-boat searched. As the darkness gathered,
its searchlight swept to and fro. Every so often they would
fire off a flare, but it was with fading hope that they continued
the search until after mid-night. All they found were some
fragments of wood which might or might not have come from
Donald's boat. They were smeared with black tar, as was the
'Helen'. But, there again, so were most of the small fishing

craft on the west coast.

Towards mid-night, clad once more in his now dry clothes, Donald stumbled through the dark to the highest point on the Eilean Dubh. In the far distance, three or more miles away, he could see the occasional flare and the flicker of the life-boat's search-light but it was far too far for him to signal, even if he had something to signal with. With a heavy heart, knowing the agony of anxiety that Ishbel would be going through, he returned to the croft.

Dod called off the search for the night around 3am. As 'Countess' slipped into Strathquinnan, he could see the hunched form of Ishbel waiting on the pier, David McPhail standing beside her.

"Nothing, I'm afraid," Dod said as came ashore. "Simply no trace. Try not to worry. He may simply have had an engine break-down and be sitting the night out somewhere waiting for day-light."

Ishbel nodded mutely and turned away.

"You don't really believe that, do you?" asked McPhail quietly.

"It doesn't look good. There's just a chance he might be okay and I don't think we should rob the poor girl of hope just yet. We'll resume the search at first light."

McPhail nodded his agreement and the two parted. McLean went home and tried to get some rest. McLeod and he went back a long way. Shared hardships and dangers forge immensely strong links between such men. He did manage to eat something, but long before dawn he, and the other crew members were back at the boat, anxious to be off.

Donald McLeod too was waiting for the dawn. By the light of a burning fence post, he had explored the barn. The last occupants had obviously reared chickens and a pile of damp straw rose to some five feet at the far end. The roof-timbers were rotten and the rain had come in here and there. As he looked, a plan began to form in Donald's mind. At the first sign of the life-boat, or any boat for that matter, he would torch the barn!

He returned to the cottage and, with great difficulty, he dragged first the table then the bed out and into the barn. Then, as the first thin light of dawn started to lighten the eastern sky, he went back to the shore-line and started to accumulate more wood. Down at the small jetty, he found four very old and decayed car tyres which had once served as fenders. These would make a lovely black smoke. He rolled them up to the barn.

When he felt he had enough fuel in the barn to ensure that the roof-timbers would catch, he climbed up to his vantage point and looked east-wards towards Strathquinnan. After over an hour, he caught sight of the orange superstructure of the life-boat, still searching two or three miles too far eastwards. He dashed down to the cottage, grabbed a burning fence-post from the fire and hurried into the barn. He thrust the post into the driest of the straw and watched with satisfaction as the fire spread. In seconds, he had to evacuate as the choking smoke filled the building. He returned up the small hill and looked back at the fire and then at the distant life-boat. The fire was, at first, disappointing. The smoke billowed out the door and window, but spread along the ground instead of rising vertically in the air. Then a flicker of flame appeared at the roof-ridge. The tongues of flame licked up through the broken slates. More slates burst explosively in the heat and then, suddenly with a crash, a major part of the roof fell in and the flames shot skywards. A foul cloud of oily black smoke from the tyres billowed upwards, driven by the convection currents high into the sky above the island.

Donald looked eastwards. Surely the life-boat crew must see the smoke. For what seemed an age, the life-boat continued to search the main-land shore. Then it seemed to disappear altogether. Suddenly, Donald realised this was because it had turned towards him and, bows-on, it was difficult to spot. Gradually, 'Countess' drew nearer. He could see, first the orange of the superstructure, then the rich, deep blue of the hull, a lovely boat at any time but of unparalleled beauty to anyone awaiting rescue. He stood on the hill-top and raised and lowered his arms until he was sure he had been seen. Then he made his way to the jetty. Cautiously, Dod McLean nosed the bows in, there being just enough water for the boat to come in. Seconds before the bows might nudge the stone-work, the engines went astern and the boat stopped. Donald leapt the two-foot gap and Dod took her out stern-first into deep water.

Donald slipped down into the cockpit and opened his mouth to speak. Only a croak emerged. Then, and only then, did he realise how utterly parched he was. There had been no drinking water on the island and the fact that he had taken more than a mouthful of sea-water when 'Helen' went down did not help. However, he was soon being feted with hot cocoa laced with rum and feeling very much the better of it.

Chapter 19

There was great rejoicing in Strathquinnan when the 'Countess' berthed and the news spread like wild-fire that Donald McLeod was safe and well. The following Sunday saw a larger than usual attendance at each of the town's churches and there was a genuine spirit of thanksgiving in the air. Even Dr Anderson was there at the parish church, something that Strathquinnan but rarely saw. Donald and Ishbel were also there, in the pew they occupied each Sunday and, after the service, Donald lingered to speak to the Rev Mike Dixon.

"Could I see you sometime?" Donald asked. "There's something I want to ask if you'd help me with."

"Of course," was the reply. "Any time. Would you like to tell me now?"

"Well, no. Not with all these people around. It's a rather private matter, you understand."

"Very well, then. How about tomorrow evening in the vestry, say about seven?"

"Fine! I'm really grateful. I'll see you then."

Dixon walked back to his manse thoughtfully. Was it some spiritual experience the life-boat coxswain had had on that island? Or, perhaps something from this morning's sermon? Mentally, he ran over the various points of the sermon. Had he said something particularly brilliant? Or something puzzling? Over the next twenty-four hours these thoughts chased one another through the minister's brain.

The following evening, he met with Donald in the vestry.

"Anything we say here will be strictly between the two of us, won't it?" began Donald.

"Yes, of course!" said Mike, starting to dread what fearful revelation might be forth-coming.

"Well, it's like this. When you sent in your CV before you took the job here, you said you were at St Andrew's University?"

"Aye!" replied the minister, intrigued and mystified at the same time.

"And that you swam in the University swimming team? Well, I wondered if you would teach me to swim."

Mike's face was a study! Whatever he had been expecting it was not this. His jaw dropped and he groped for words. Before he could gather his thoughts the life-boat man went on.

"You know none of us can swim. Well, there was me, in easy swimming distance of Eilean Dubh but, if I hadn't grabbed that plank, I'd have drowned. Ishbel would be a widow and my lads fatherless. It seemed pretty stupid to me not to learn, seeing I've been given a second chance, so to speak. I hope you don't mind me asking?"

"No, no, of course not. I'll give you all the help I can.

Of course I will! But why the secrecy?"

"Fishermen don't swim and I don't want the other fellows to know. They'll think I've gone soft or something."

Mike laughed. "You're all daft! You're missing out on a great sport. You're putting your own lives in unnecessary danger. And one day, you might just have to stand back and watch someone drown simply because you can't swim. When do you want to start?"

"As soon as you like. Early morning'll be best. We could use one of the pools up the Quinnan. No-one'll be up there early on."

Mike thought quickly. The River Quinnan would be freezing! At this time of year it was probably still being fed with snow-melt on the high-tops. However, the fellow was serious and he felt he could not let him down.

"Tomorrow, then?" he asked with a counterfeit enthusiasm.

"Great!" said Donald rising to go. "Thanks again. I really do appreciate this." And he left.

"I wonder if you realise how cold it's going to be," mused the minister, after Donald had gone. Then he remembered that Donald had much more recent experience of cold water than Mike himself had.

The days that followed were tough for Mike. The Quinnan was every bit as cold as he had expected but Donald's mind was made up. He was going to learn to swim and that was that. Indeed, he was a really keen pupil and soon was swimming reasonably competently.

All went well until one day the two were swimming in

one of the bigger salmon pools when they heard approaching voices. Peering over the bank, Mike was horrified to see the laird, Sir Torquil McNab, walking up the path with one of his ghillies.

"Get your head down," hissed Donald. "I'll be the laughing-stock of Strathquinnan if it gets out that I've been learning to swim!"

"And what about me?" whispered Mike. "If he gets it into his head that we've been guddling his trout, I'll be out of a job! And I'll be the laughing-stock of the tabloid press all

93

over Scotland, never mind Strathquinnan!"

The two friends crouched under the bank where the stream had under-cut it. Chest-deep in the freezing water they waited for what seemed an eternity. At length, the Laird and his man moved on and the pair slid like otters out of the water and into the bracken where their towels and clothes were.

"If I catch a cold, I'll announce from the pulpit that you've been learning to swim!" said Mike through his chattering teeth.

"Do that, and I'll say that we weren't swimming. We were just poaching trout!"

"Okay! Truce! We'll both say nothing, but that was a lucky shave. I'm just glad I not standing here trying to explain the situation to Sir Torquil!"

Chapter 20

Irene McGregor arrived home from work, happily humming to herself and blissfully unaware of the storm that was about to be unleashed upon her. Her mother had suddenly decided to do some spring-cleaning. That was how she came to open the drawer where Irene's brown paper-covered book lay concealed. Intrigued, she drew it out and opened it at the title page. She went ashen as her eyes fell upon the print. Her hands trembled as she read. "The New Testament. A Modern Translation by J.B. Phillips."

Horrified, she dashed through to the kitchen, flung open the door of the Aga stove and thrust the offending book into the flames. Then she went over to the sink and scrubbed her hands. Still shaking, she sat down, tears in her eyes. How could a daughter of hers read such a book? It would break her husband's heart. Where had they gone wrong? They had done all they could to bring their girl up in the true faith and this was how she rewarded them! So, simmering gently, she awaited Irene's return.

As Irene entered the pent-up storm broke.

"How could you? How could you? Do you want to bring your poor father to an early grave? It would break his heart if he learnt that a daughter of his had such a book in her possession. Indeed, he must never know. I can only guess what the shock might do to him!"

"But mother," wailed Irene. "I only wanted to understand the Bible better. Can that be so wrong?"

"Understand the Bible! That wretched book's not the Bible. You've got the Bible up beside your bed. If that was good enough for St Paul and St Peter, good enough for Calvin and Knox, surely it's good enough for you. Besides, if you can't understand anything, you can aye ask your father or one of the Men at the church."

Recognising the uselessness of further discussion, Irene withdrew to her room, threw herself on the bed and wept. After several minutes, she pulled herself together and slipped out the back door of the house. Along the sea-shore, she collected her thoughts. Could it really be so wrong to wish to understand the Scriptures? Did her father and the Men at the Free Presbyterian Church really have a monopoly of the truth? Was there indeed any real difference in her having to go to her father for the Bible to be explained than for a Catholic to have to go to a priest? Yet these sectarian differences continued to drive wedges between the Strathquinnan society. Somehow, despite all her upbringing, she could not bring herself to believe that that was what God wanted. And what about Shug? Her fiancé had been brought up in the Church of Scotland, but in recent months had been attending the Free Presbyterian church with her. Was he merely tolerated by her father because, if he became at least an adherent, if not a full member, it would be a feather in the old man's cap? Yet, to fall out with the family would be final. Did she really want to turn her back on her parents and all they held dear? The poor girl was in an unanswerable quandary.

The one acceptable way for Irene to escape from the oppressively suffocating atmosphere at home was marriage. Inwardly, she determined that her wedding day was going to be as early as decency and finance would permit.

Chapter 21

Irene McGregor was not the only one in Strathquinnan who found the deeply entrenched stance of the various members of the towns religious community frustrating. Mike Dixon, looking back over the months he had been parish minister in Strathquinnan, felt both disappointed and something of personal failure. One evening, he shared his thoughts with Dr Anderson.

"I don't know if I'm simply the wrong man for this town or what! Everybody is very courteous and no one contradicts anything I say, but I just seem unable to get through to them."

The doctor looked at him with a kindly smile. "Never forget," he said, "these people are very slow to reveal what they are thinking, especially about their religious beliefs. Oh! They'll parrot all the standard slogans of their own particular church, right enough, but that's no indication of what they really think. The one thing you can be sure of is that the more profoundly moved they are by anything you preach, the less likely they will be to let you know that you've touched them at all. The best you can hope for by way of approbation is a firm handshake at the church door. If you're lucky you might get a growl which you think you can interpret as thanks, but you're not sure!"

"It's not just that," replied Mike. "I'm not looking for a pat on the back. I want these people to be happily secure in the belief that God loves them and that he will receive them, forgiving them freely. The trouble is that they have these firmly held convictions that God's love must be earned. They just refuse to accept that that attitude is totally contrary to all the teaching of Jesus."

"Aye, well, you're up against the Protestant work ethic. They firmly believe that a man should work for everything he wants. They're utterly opposed to a 'something-for-nothing' attitude. That makes your job difficult, to say the least. You're telling them that God will forgive them freely because Christ has died for them and they're sitting there thinking 'Yes, but we must also keep the Sabbath, be honest, be kind and so on.' You've a tough job on your hands! These ancient traditions are so deep-seated that altering attitudes which have been passed down from one generation to the next is so difficult as to be virtually impossible."

"You can say that again!" Mike replied warmly. "What upsets me most is that it makes such a nonsense of the Communion services. The church is packed on Communion Sundays with people who seem to think that they are earning merit by attending. The whole point of the Sacrament is that it's supposed to emphasise the fact that Christ died to take away our sins. Yet, instead of rejoicing in forgiveness as free gift from a God who loves them, these poor souls are struggling to try to win a pardon from a rather cold and distant God who seems more like a judge than a Heavenly Father. What makes it even worse is that attendance at Communion is thought to be just another way of winning God's approval."

"I can understand your frustration. However, all you can do is to keep on keeping on. You may be having more effect than you think. I tell you, the one thing you can be sure of is that these folk would sooner walk across the square stark naked than expose their innermost souls to you or anyone else! You'll just have to learn to live with that!"

Chapter 22

There was little drama to the next call-out of the Strathquinnan boat. Certainly there was no intimation of the danger that lay ahead for both boat and crew. A telephone call from the coastguard reported a freighter on fire off Ardnamurchan point. The 'Countess' slipped her moorings with a full crew and headed westwards in calm seas. Long before they caught sight of the Liberian registered 'Captain Robson', the lifeboatmen could see the pillar of black smoke to the west. From the coastguard, Donald McLeod had learned that the 'Captain Robson' was bound for Stornoway with a mixed cargo that included paint, turpentine and tractor fuel. A fire in her engine room had left her helpless. It had spread to her fuel tanks, but not, as yet, to her cargo hold. This was heating up steadily however as the rapidly increasing temperature was conducted throughout the hull.

The captain had rather belatedly given the order to abandon ship. One of the two lifeboats had got away, but the other was hopelessly tangled up and hung, almost vertically, its bows pointing uselessly to the sky. The unfortunate members of crew who were not in the ship's boat were clinging to a Carley float under the stern of the vessel. Their comrades managed to get a line to them and were bending to the oars to try to put some distance between themselves and the stricken ship.

This was the scene as Donald McLeod and his crew found it. Approaching the ship's life-boat and the Carley float, the Strathquinnan men felt the intense heat of the burning freighter on their faces. The ship was a fairly old one, with a raised bow and stern, the bridge and funnel being mid-ships. The whole of this central part was ablaze, the steel plates glowing a cherry-red down to within a couple of feet of the water-line.

Donald took in the scene at a glance and brought 'Countess' in at full speed under the freighter's stern. Cutting the engines, he swung the life-boat in alongside the float. As the two closed, he put the engines astern and shouted for the sailors to jump, which they did with a will. The fumes from the time-bomb of a ship alongside and above them were nearly overpowering. There was no time to think about towing the ship's lifeboat to safety. A quick jab with the throttles and 'Countess' was alongside it. The grateful survivors scrambled aboard, being hauled enthusiastically to safety by 'Countess's' crew. As soon as the last survivor was aboard, the throttles of the life-boat were thrust wide open and the gap between the two vessels began to widen.

Just as Donald began to relax, there was the most almighty explosion behind them. A ball of flame surged from the freighter's forward hold. It shot upwards for hundreds of feet, and outwards, almost reaching the life-boat. The abandoned ship's lifeboat was lost in the spreading inferno. A

gust of super-heated air swept over 'Countess'. Each man felt the searing heat strike his face like a physical bow. Each gasped in the oxygen-starved atmosphere. Each smelt the peculiar smell of his hair being singed. Then it was past.

The pillar of smoke from the 'Captain Robson' was now a pillar of fire, with flames shooting sky-wards, carrying blazing debris high into the air, to fall back into the sea on all sides of the ship. The blaze was accompanied by a steady roar like a jet engine, punctuated with periodic explosions as some new barrel of flammable liquid made its contribution to the inferno. Donald muttered, "I think it's time we went home, boys." With that he set a course for Strathquinnan.

Shouting for Dod to check for injury or damage to the craft, Donald prayed a secret prayer. "Please, Lord, please may I not have to go back to Strathquinnan by bus!"

Dod reported back. The boat was unscathed. All who had been on deck were scorched and had their hair or their beards or their eyelashes singed, in some cases all three. But no-one was seriously hurt. All felt their faces burning as though they had been too long in the sun, but, apart from that, there seemed to be no permanent damage.

"A close-run thing! A close-run thing!" Donald muttered repeatedly to Dod. He knew he had taken an appalling risk bringing the 'Countess' so close to the doomed freighter. He gripped the wheel firmly to conceal just how much his hands were shaking. How he would be feeling now if any of his men had died or been severely injured, he had no real idea. What he was sure of was that not a man among them would have wished him to have hung off at a safe distance whilst they watched the cremation of the 'Captain Robson's' crew.

Donald took the decision to head straight for Oban where the hospital had comprehensive accident and emergency facilities, even though Strathquinnan was much nearer. He radioed his intentions and four hours later 'Countess' was moored up against Oban pier. Later that evening, each man having received medical treatment, she slipped her moorings and headed home.

Chapter 23

David McPhail took his duties as life-boat secretary very seriously. Ever since the near-disaster when the 'Countess' had capsized, he had maintained a steady campaign for a newer and better boat for Strathquinnan. At times he felt his pleas were falling on deaf ears. However, he did understand the on-going problems of the RNLI. Contrary to what most people thought, the Lifeboat Institute was not funded by taxation. All the funds it received were from the general public and there never seemed to be enough to go round.

No doubt, up and down the country, there were other local secretaries and lifeboat committees that felt just as strongly as did McPhail that their particular boat should be up-dated. McPhail at times reflected that he himself would not like to be the one to make the decision about which boat should be stationed where. However, he felt his own duty clear. Strathquinnan's men deserved the best and he, McPhail, would fight as hard as he could to get it for them.

For all that, it came as a great surprise when he learned that spring that, at last, his tenacity was being rewarded. Strathquinnan had been allocated a brand new boat. Late that summer, Donald McLeod and four other crew members took the train from Oban and went to Cockenzie to take over the new craft which a passage crew had brought up from the Solent. By the time the five men had worked the boat up the east coast of Scotland, through the Caledonian Canal and down to Strathquinnan, they were thoroughly familiar with the craft and every one of them was wildly enthusiastic about it.

There was, of course, a naming ceremony. The harbour was decked out with flags. The end of the pier with the best view was roped off and seats from the village hall were set out for visiting dignitaries. The school children were given the day off and a holiday atmosphere prevailed throughout the town. A small platform was erected for the VIPs and, especially, for the Duchess who was to name the new boat. A public address system, with speakers dangling from lamp-posts round the harbour was to ensure that all who attended would hear every word.

The great day dawned with a thick, white fog obscuring everything, it being impossible to see even across the harbour. However, as the morning wore on, the sun burned off the mist and the afternoon was bright and warm. The new boat was moored alongside the pier, dressed from bow to stern with bunting. Everything was ready and the platform party, having had a hearty lunch at the Crown, made their dignified way to the pier. Mike Dixon, as honorary chaplain to the crew, was to have a prominent part in the proceedings, dedicating the lifeboat to the preservation of life at sea.

So the ceremony got under way. The pier was

thronged as practically the entire population of Strathquinnan and the surrounding area was there. Those who could not get on the pier straggled round the other three sides of the harbour. After initial speeches, Mike was introduced and began the religious part of the ceremony. The singing of the sailors' hymn, 'Eternal Father, strong to save', was an unmitigated disaster. The sound system carried the amplified singing of the church choir across the harbour, but the time-lag due to the distance involved meant that those on the pier were half a line ahead of those on the other side. But for the solemnity of the occasion, the result would have been laughable. However, with due dignity, the choir laboured on and eventually reached the final lines

>'From rock and tempest, fire and foe,
>Protect them wheresoe'er they go;
>Thus ever more shall rise to Thee
>Glad hymns of praise from land and sea.'

Mike then read Psalm 107, the sailors' Psalm.

"They that go down to the sea in ships, that do business in great waters; these see the works of the Lord and his wonders in the deep......"

He had barely started when there was a cry and a splash. A child, anxious to get a better view had been squeezing past the adults around him and had overbalanced, entering the water fifteen feet or so behind the lifeboat.

"Donald!" shouted Mike. Donald McLeod was

stationed in the cockpit of the new boat. In a trice, he was over the side and swimming strongly to where the kid had disappeared into the water. He did a beautiful duck-dive and he too disappeared for what seemed minutes but was, in fact, only seconds. He emerged with the child firmly in his grasp and swam on to the nearest stairway where eager hands pulled the boy to safety. Dr Anderson pushed his way through the crowd, examined the lad and pronounced him fine.

A sigh of relief swept through the crowd. Donald shinned down a vertical ladder and resumed his position in the cockpit. A stunned silence followed. Every eye was on the still-dripping coxswain. A Strathquinnan fisherman who could swim! Indeed, if Donald had rescued the boy by walking across the top of the water, that would have been only slightly more miraculous!

Hiding a smile, Mike brought the crowd's attention back to the purpose of the day's proceedings and resumed his reading. Later that evening, as so often before, he met up with Dr Anderson for a quiet chat over supper.

"Well! It seems the age of miracles is not yet past! Where ever did Donny McLeod learn to swim like that? It's certainly since his adventures on Eilean Dubh. I wouldn't have believed it had I not seen it with my own eyes! It'll be the talk of the town, I can tell you!"

The doctor peered over his half-moon glasses at the young minister. "By the by, why was it Donald and none of the others you shouted to?"

"My lips are sealed," replied Mike with a grin. "As you say, the days of miracles are not over!"

The doctor continued, "Why these men won't learn to swim, I'll never know! With the older generation, I used to think it was a natural aversion to anything which remotely resembled washing! You wouldn't know, but a long time back, long before you came, one of the lobster men drowned. He was pulling up a pot. Presumably the line snagged and a freak wave hit his boat at the same time. Anyway, he plopped over the stern, his feet accidentally pushing the boat from him. There was another boat less than a hundred yards away and they saw everything. The poor fellow surfaced momentarily. There was his boat a mere six feet or so away, but he couldn't swim a stroke. The others rowed over as fast as they could. He slipped under when they were only twenty yards away. His body was washed up on the west sands a fortnight later."

The old man paused, deep in sad thoughts. Then he resumed.

"As I say, that was back in the early fifties. I tried to get a campaign going to encourage at least all the younger fishermen to learn to swim, but would they? Then I bought a whole batch of war-surplus life-jackets from Gamages. I got them for a song and distributed them round the town. Again, would they wear them? No chance! Seemed to think it was namby-pamby to be seen in such a thing. Said it impeded their movements. Lifejackets dashed well didn't seem to impede the commandos streaming ashore at Normandy with their rucksacks and rifles! Nor did those lads think they were namby-pamby! It's years since I saw one of the life-jackets and then it was being used as a fender on a yawl!"

"That's just so typical of Strathquinnan!" replied Mike. "I can never make up my mind whether these people have deep faith and believe that God will bring them safely through all dangers, or whether they are just fatalists who believe and accept that the future is already unalterably mapped out for them."

"A little bit of both, I imagine," said the doctor. "That, and stubbornness. Thrawn! That's what these people are! Thrawn!"

Mike smiled. The English language was rich in words to express each point of view. Had the doctor approved of the fishing folks attitude, he would have described it as 'principled' or 'strong-willed'. However, 'thrawn' summed them up and, at the same time adequately expressed their doctor's opinion of them!

Chapter 24

The new lifeboat was soon in action. The first call-out came in late August. It was to search for a yacht with three men and a woman on board. The four were from a party of three couples who were on a yachting holiday, sailing in the waters around Tobermory. Two of the husbands plus one couple had set out to visit the Island of Staffa to see Fingal's Cave. That would take the 25 foot boat well out into the exposed waters of the Minch. The wind had been blowing a steady force three from the south-west when they left but had freshened as the day wore on, swinging to the north-west. At nightfall, when there was no sign of the yacht returning, the wives who had remained behind raised the alarm.

Strathquinnan's new lifeboat, the 'Diana', set out just after mid-night. It was too dark for any realistic searching to commence, but, as the dawn broke, she was well out in the Minch and ready to join in a systematic search along with her sister boats from Oban and Mallaig. Two of the boats concentrated on the shore-line, the one patrolling the waters off the Ardnamurchan peninsular and the north-west coast of the island of Mull, the other working farther south around the Island of Ulva and the other islands and reefs along the west coast of Mull. Meanwhile Strathquinnan's 'Diana' headed into the force five winds and rising seas towards Staffa and the Treshnish Isles.

"If they've foundered, it'll be a miracle if we find anything," muttered Donald pessimistically. "They're said to be well-equipped with a life-raft and lifejackets, but they'll be nearly impossible to spot unless we get within a few hundred yards of them."

"They may, of course, be lying storm-bound in one of Mull's sea-lochs. Apparently the yacht has a small in-board engine but, if they were being swept inshore, it might not have had the power to keep them in deep water. They'd then have to anchor off and ride it out. All right, provided their anchor holds," said Tam Ross who was standing beside him.

"If they're anchored off somewhere, the coastguards'll find them. They called out all the Auxiliaries and every yard of the shore-line will have been patrolled before noon. We'll hear soon enough if they find them. Likewise, the coastguards will have their eyes peeled for any wreckage on the beaches. The big risk is that the boat capsized and sank. That would give no chance for the crew to take to the life-raft. If they had their life-jackets on and managed to get clear of the wreck, they could perhaps survive for twenty-four hours in the water at this time of year, but certainly no more. The trouble is that they'd be so hard to spot unless we were lucky enough to come within yards of them."

The early afternoon found the 'Diana' doing a box search eight miles or so east of Tiree. The crew were positioned round the boat, each raking the seas with binoculars. The wind was blowing steadily from the north-west but the currents tended to sweep south-east. Even if the lifeboat coxswain had known precisely where the missing boat had gone down, calculating where any survivors might have drifted to was sheer guess-work.

A large trawler appeared to the west so Donald headed over to it. It was a neglected-looking craft with rust-streaks down its filthy hull. About 150 feet in length, it bristled with radio masts and antenna.

"A commie spy-ship!" said Dod.

At this stage in the cold-war, the Russians had large fishing fleets operating in international waters off the Scottish coast. These were quite legitimately carrying out their trawling operations. What was more questionable was why some of them, like the ship before them now, carried so much radio gear. The accepted explanation was that these were the spy-ships sent under cover of the perfectly legal fishing fleet to carry out the less legal monitoring of NATO submarines and other vessels in and around the approaches to the Clyde naval bases. The British Government no doubt had ample reason to make a complaint about the blatant incursions into their waters, but perhaps did not do so because the consequent uproar might further worsen east-west relations, never good at the best of times.

'Diana' was now in hailing distance of the Russian vessel. Donald raised his megaphone and called up the other ship. The only answer was an incomprehensible stream of what was, presumably, Russian. Patiently, he tried again, explaining the object of their search. Still no reply in English.

"Surely there must be someone on that crate that understands English!" Tam exclaimed angrily.

"Oh! They do! Of that I'm sure," Donald replied. "It's just that they don't want to co-operate with the British. That's all. The Russians haven't got a ship like that lying off our coasts to monitor radio transmissions from our Navy without any of the crew knowing English! My bet is that even the ship's cook knows and understands every word I've said. Well, we're wasting our time here. Better get on with the next leg of our search." And he swung the wheel round and headed eastwards once more.

By 9pm, the daylight was fading fast and, rather reluctantly, Donald called off the search for the night. An exchange of radio messages confirmed that the other two lifeboats were doing likewise. Rather than make the longer trip to base, all three would lie up for the night in Tobermory where the crew could rest and the boats be refuelled. As the 'Diana' slipped passed Calf Island and into the shelter of Tobermory bay, the crew could see the other two boats were there before them. Drawing near the pier, they saw a huddle of strained faces watching their approach.

"The wives and relatives," murmured Donald. "How I hate coming in with bad news, or, as tonight, with no news."

He scrambled up the ladder and was met by a couple of young women, each with red eyes and faces creased with worry. Sadly, he shook his head.

"No news. I'm sorry, but we've found nothing."

One of the women burst into tears. The other threw an arm round her friend.

Donald, hunting for something to say, went on, "Don't give up hope. It's a huge area we're searching and there's still a chance that they're marooned on a skerry or island somewhere. We'll put to sea before first light and, who knows, we may be lucky tomorrow."

The women left and Donald stood silently on the pier. Was he being an utter hypocrite? Was it right to hold out any hope? A wave of sadness swept over him. He was no coward. He had braved the elements on countless occasions. But he was terrified that he might be back here tomorrow night, on the same pier, telling the same two women that there husbands were gone for ever.

The following morning, as the first rays of sunlight were starting to lighten the sky in the north-east, the three lifeboats left Tobermory. It had been decided that the assumption must be that the yacht had foundered somewhere between Ardnamurchan and Staffa and therefore any survivors would have drifted towards Mull itself. The lifeboats would patrol the sea and search the off-shore reefs and skerries whilst the coastguards, aided by volunteers, would again sweep the shore-line looking for survivors, bodies or wreckage.

Keeping station in line abreast, the lifeboats rounded the north-west tip of Mull and then sailed southwards. The Mallaig boat swung eastwards to search north of the Island of Ulva, the Oban boat set off to search the south shore of Ulva and its associated islands and reefs, whilst 'Diana' continued south towards Iona. Moving in close to the island, Donald steered east-wards, passing Iona's northern shore and then searching along the peninsular known as the Ross of Mull. Early in the afternoon, came a radio message. A body had been found on a low-lying reef off Ulva. That gave new direction to the search and 'Diana' swung north to join the other two boats. All three would now concentrate on the southern side of Ulva and the seas off it. However, before 'Diana' had reached the search area, more tragic news followed. Another body was recovered and, soon after that, the remaining two. There was nothing left to do but to return to base.

A deep gloom descended on 'Diana's' crew. An unjustified sense of having failed was the unspoken feeling among them. Each man knew they had done all that could have been done. Indeed the yacht's crew may have perished even before the lifeboat had been called out, but still their over-riding emotion was that of having somehow let others down.

"At least we don't have to go back to Tobermory," mused Donald sadly, as he remembered the haunting looks of anxiety and grief on the two women's faces. Late that evening 'Diana' having been refuelled and safely moored at her pontoon berth, the crew dispersed silently into the dusk.

Chapter 25

A rather uneventful autumn followed. 'Diana' was twice called out. Once was to escort a local fishing boat that was taking water. However, in the event, the boat's own pumps held until the vessel was safely beached on the harbour slip, ready for repair when the tide ebbed. The second was even less dramatic. A man had fallen overboard from one of the inter-island ferries. However, while 'Diana' was still less than half-way to the scene, the news came that a fishing boat had picked him up, rather surprisingly suffering from nothing more than mild exposure and cold.

Then the winter set in. December opened with unremitting wind and rain. By the beginning of the second week, the fishing fleets throughout Scotland which had returned home for the week-end were storm-bound. The Monday had started off blustery and, with severe gales forecast for almost every sea-area, the Strathquinnan boats stayed tied up at the pier. By early afternoon, the decision not to sail was more than amply justified. By late evening, the wind was lifting slates off roofs and tearing branches from trees. Despite the fact that the men-folk who would normally be at sea were at home, Strathquinnan was strangely dead.

The few who ventured out on Tuesday did so with heads down and coats clasped firmly round them.

Early that Tuesday afternoon, Irene McGregor was hurrying along the main street with head well down and the wind in her teeth. Ahead of her was the harbour, the fishing boats, though sheltered by the pier, straining at their moorings as they pitched up and down. At regular intervals, a wave larger than its fellows, would break right over the pier in a fountain of white spray. She licked her lips and, even at that distance, could taste the sea-salt on them. Suddenly she overheard a scrap of conversation from a couple sheltering in a door-way. Her heart stopped.

"Aye, all the lifeboat crew lost. The boat was called out about three this morning and they've found her washed up ashore. No survivors."

A terrible wave of agony swept over Irene, to be followed in turn by a wave of relief as she looked up and saw 'Diana' tossing at her pontoon mooring. The Strathquinnan boat and its crew were safe! Then relief gave way to guilt. Her relief that Shug had not been taken meant somewhere else sweet-hearts, wives, parents, and children had been struck by the very disaster she had feared. She turned into the shelter of the shop-doorway.

"Did I hear you say a lifeboat has been lost?"

"Aye, lass. I'm sorry, but it's true. I heard it on the Home Service lunch-time news. A place called Broughty Ferry, somewhere on the east coast. Eight good men gone. And some poor woman's lost both her husband and her son."

Irene mumbled her thanks and, with her eyes welling

with tears, she hurried off again. What if it had been Strathquinnan? She thought of the number of grieving families such a disaster would produce. They all lived with this kind of fear every time the boat was called out. The whole country would no doubt grieve for the bereaved of Broughty Ferry, but it was surely only in lifeboat towns and villages that there would be those who would have some inkling of the real agonies of the stricken families and community.

By evening, when every living soul in Strathquinnan except the very youngest had listened to the Six o'clock News, much more detail was known. The 'Mona', a 45 foot Watson boat, had been launched in the early hours of Tuesday 8th December to go to the aid of a light-ship that was dragging its anchors and was in imminent danger of being cast up on the rugged rocks of Fife Ness. The 'Mona' had remained in radio contact as she left Broughty Ferry, a one-time fishing village, but now a suburb of Dundee. The storm was at its height but she reported that she had safely crossed the notoriously dangerous bar at the mouth of the River Tay. After that, despite continued attempts to contact her by both the Fife and the Carnoustie coastguards, there were no more messages by radio. At first light an air and sea-search began but soon ended when news came that the wreck of the 'Mona' had been washed ashore on Buddon Ness. With the boat were the bodies of seven of her crew of eight. The only good news was that the light-ship had been able to get out an anchor that was holding, but only just. The crew had been plucked to safety from the ship by helicopter.

The following days brought more news, all testimony

to the extreme violence of the weather. The storm that had taken the brave men of Broughty Ferry had wreaked terrible havoc elsewhere. A small coaster, the 'Servus', had lost all power 26 miles north-east of Lossiemouth in the Moray Firth. The Cromarty lifeboat had gone to her aid, but the howling gales swept the coaster on to Dunbeath Head, some twenty miles south of Wick. The Cromarty boat's coxswain, with nearly incredible courage and skill, had brought the lifeboat close enough to the wreck to rescue her crew of eight.

Farther south, the Scandinavian registered 'Anna' was wrecked on rocks off St Combs, ten miles south of Fraserburgh. Neither the Fraserburgh nor the Peterhead lifeboats could be launched, such was the severity of the storm. Before the Cromarty boat could be brought to the scene of the action, the complete crew of the 'Anna', 16 in all, had been rescued by breeches buoy from the cliff-top. Less fortunate were the crew of a German and of a Norwegian freighter. Both ships went down with all hands, a total of 27 men being lost with the two vessels.

Among the crew and committee of the Strathquinnan lifeboat, two decisions were taken. Strathquinnan would set up a disaster appeal for the aid of the dependants of the Broughty Ferry men. And Strathquinnan would be represented at the memorial service at Broughty Ferry. David McPhail would go, taking his car. Donald McLean would be the natural choice to accompany him. However, McPhail was also willing to take another two as the car seats would otherwise be vacant. After much debate, it was agreed that the Fraser brothers would go.

By the Thursday, the weather had moderated and the four set off in a light drizzle. As they left the coast and started to climb Glen Coe, what rain there was turned to snow. Fortunately, as they went east, the snow went off and a sickly sun-light broke through. This was just as well for, by the time they were crossing Rannoch Moor, the snow lay thick around them. The road had been ploughed, leaving high walls of snow on each side. Clearly, very little more would be needed to fall for the road to be blocked once more. Near Lochearnhead, the lifeboatmen twice had to get out and push the car through stretches of the road where the wind had blown the drifting snow back on to the carriageway. It took fully six hours to reach Perth, where McPhail had arranged for them to spend the night with a cousin of his.

The next morning, they left Perth early to cover the last 26 mile leg of the journey to the church in time for the 11am memorial service. Just after 10am, the car made its way along the main shopping street of Broughty Ferry. The shops were shut. Houses had their blinds drawn and the full impact of the tragedy on this close-knit community began to hit the Strathquinnan men. The car had to be parked some distance from the fishermen's church which stood on the bank of the Tay immediately opposite the now vacant lifeboat shed from which the 'Mona' had been launched only three short days earlier.

Although there were still fifty minutes to go before the service began, there were already hundreds of people huddled on the east side of the street, heads bowed as flurries of hail and snow hit them. McPhail made his way to the church door. A few minutes later he returned.

"I'm sorry, but there are only three seats reserved for our delegation. There are lifeboatmen coming from stations all the way up and down the coast as well as from elsewhere, like ourselves."

The two brothers had a quick debate, then announced that Shug would go in and Chic remain outside. McPhail and the two went inside, leaving the third lifeboatman standing beside a huge police-sergeant. The man was all of six foot four and seemed to be of similar dimensions round the chest. Surreptitiously, Chic manoeuvred himself to the lee side of the big policeman and found that he made an excellent wind-break, providing more than adequate cover for Chic's slim form.

An announcement came over the loud-speaker that limited accommodation was available in the church hall and that the service would be relayed there as well as into the street. Without being asked to, the men stood back, leaving the way clear for most of the women to get in out of the blustery rain. The silence was then broken as a couple of RAF jets from the nearby station at Leuchars roared overhead. Then came a heavy squall of hail, but no-one in the crowd sought shelter.

Just before eleven, the door of the lifeboat shed opened and a small party of dignitaries emerged.

"The tall one at the front's Earl Howe," muttered the policeman to those around him. "He's the head man of the RNLI. The smaller chap behind him'll be Lord Saltoun. He's the Scottish Chairman."

About the same time the Lord Provost of Dundee arrived with a delegation from the council. Chic caught sight too of what he assumed to be the parish minister, a very tall, almost gaunt figure, his faced lined with grief.

After an interval, the service started with the singing of a Paraphrase that Chic did not know. Judging by the quality of the singing, he was one of a substantial majority. The readings and prayers washed over Chic. His mind wandered as he looked up and down the street. The rain had almost stopped and a thin sun struggled to shine bleakly through the scudding clouds. Suddenly the congregation were singing again. This time, Chic did know the tune at least. The haunting strains of Sibelius' *'Finlandia'*. He listened and the dimly remembered words hit him.

> "Be still, my soul: when dearest friends depart,
> And all is darkened in the vale of tears.
> Then shalt thou better know His love, His heart,
> Who comes to soothe thy sorrow and thy fears.
> Be still, my soul: thy Jesus can repay,
> From His own fullness, all he takes away."

Chic looked up at the tall figure who was towering over him. The policeman had removed his hat and stood bare-headed, tears unashamedly streaming down his cheeks. A flurry of rain struck, mingling with the big man's tears.

And Chic wept too.

*　　*　　*　　*　　*　　*

Inside the small church, McPhail and his two companions were squeezed into an over-crowded pew. The building was packed and there was not a dry eye anywhere. The deep emotion of the service nearly overwhelmed McPhail. The sheer horror of the tragedy left him with profound doubts about a loving and all-powerful God. The minister conducting the service prayed to such a God with what was obviously a deep and sincere faith, but McPhail found himself full of unanswered questions. Did God know? Did God care? The sermon left McPhail cold. Had God really any idea what these people were experiencing? There was that poor widow, grieving the loss, not only of a husband, but of a son too. What did God know about human suffering? Did God really know what it was like to lose a son? He looked up at the two large stained-glass windows at the front of the church. One depicted Christ, bowed under the weight of the cross he was bearing to Calvary, the cross that would shortly be bearing his body as he died there. Above the stained-glass picture were the words "Surely He has borne our griefs and carried our sorrows." Some glimmer of light seemed to reach McPhail. Perhaps, after all, God did know. Perhaps God did care.

The service over, the crowd began to disperse. With some difficulty, the Strathquinnan men met up and returned wordlessly to McPhail's Rover. Their route took them through the centre of Dundee. If Dundee, like its eastern suburb of Broughty Ferry had come to a standstill whilst the service was on, there were no signs of it now. The younger men had never been in such a large city and were somewhat awe-struck at the streets where cars and lorries, buses and horse-carts, not to mention pedestrians, competed to get a share of the limited thoroughfare. They passed the City Square where a huge Christmas tree and other decorations bade the citizens a Merry Christmas.

"There'll not be much joy in Broughty Ferry this Christmas," McPhail muttered, as much to himself as to the others.

Conversation was muted after that, even when they stopped in Crieff for a late lunch. Each man was too full of his own thoughts to want to talk. However, as the Rover purred along the side of Loch Earn, Shug remarked. "I was a little surprised that we didn't sing the sailors' hymn. You know, 'Eternal Father, strong to save.'"

"Perhaps we should be singing it when the seas are calm, not just keeping it in reserve for when things go wrong," said McPhail thoughtfully.

He drove on in silence, his mind going back nearly twenty years to the Malta convoys. Well did he remember standing watch in the darkness of the Mediterranean night, humming that very hymn repeatedly. He hummed it now

"O Trinity of love and power,
Our brethren shield in danger's hour;
From rock and tempest, fire and foe
Protect them wheresoe'er they go.
Thus ever more shall rise to Thee
Glad hymns of praise from land and sea."

The familiar words transported him back in time and back to the deck of an old destroyer as he watched for the tell-tale sign of a surface raider's bow-wave creaming towards them or the yet more stealthy approach of a submarine. He remembered the pillars of fire that would suddenly erupt in the night as a cargo-ship or, worse still, a tanker, was struck by a torpedo. He remembered the gun-fire, the depth-charging, the dragging of pathetic survivors from the water. A shudder went through him. More than fifteen years ago, and his sleep was still so often tortured by these memories.

Chapter 26

The two weeks between the Broughty Ferry visit and Christmas celebrations passed with what seemed to be improper speed for McPhail. He recognised that the children of Strathquinnan should not have their happiness blighted by the very real sorrow that every adult in the village felt. However, as the Christmas Eve Carol Service began on Thursday evening, he found himself wishing he had some valid reason for absenting himself. The children were excited and happy and their parents were making a good job of hiding their inner sadness. However, McPhail knew that there was not a man or woman among them who was not wondering what sort of Christmas it would be in that still-stunned east-coast town.

McPhail settled down in a back corner of the church, glad that the building was lit more by candles than by the usual bright electric lights. His eyes welled with tears as children's piping voices sung the old, familiar carols. As the service progressed, with the well-known Bible readings interspersed with the even better known hymns, it became clear to him as perhaps never before that the whole of the Christian faith rested on the proposition summed up in this service - that God has revealed himself by visiting this world as a man - Jesus. If true, the implications were mind-boggling. If false, the whole thing was an empty charade. If true, there was hope for a future after death. If false, there was nothing.

As the service drew to its close, McPhail found himself challenged by the closing carol:

No ear may hear his coming;
but in this world of sin,
where meek souls will receive him, still
the dear Christ enters in.
O Holy Child of Bethlehem
descend to us we pray;
cast out our sin and enter in;
be born in us to-day.

Dare he take this seriously? Dare he pray this and, if he did, what would happen? Long after the congregation had dispersed, the solicitor sat in his seat in the now dark church, feeling that he was on the verge of a life-changing experience.

Chapter 27

Lizzie Stewart was bored. Al was away on a five-day fishing trip. As usual, nothing very much was happening in Strathquinnan. Increasingly, Lizzie day-dreamed about starting a new life in a big city where things really did happen, where there were cinemas and where there were dance-halls. The monotony of her unhappy little world in Strathquinnan was becoming unbearable.

Her secret fund was building up, though not so fast as in the days of the unlamented Angus Wallace. She still worked regularly part-time at the hotel, but the opportunities of supplementing her wages there were sadly limited. Whenever she could, Lizzie went with her brother-in-law, Ewan Stewart, to Oban on his visits to the meat-market. The two had slipped into a comfortable routine of stopping at a secluded semi-derelict croft, ostensibly for tea from her thermos. Glen Duchally, where the croft was, had once supported three or four families. However, first the coming of sheep, then more recently, the blanketing of whole hill-sides with larch and pine trees had left it deserted and, to all intents and purposes, forgotten. This desolation made the croft a secure, if not very comfortable, stopping-point on the road back from Oban. These encounters were not particularly exciting or sexually satisfying for Lizzie, but they were sufficiently enjoyable for Ewan to ensure that her weekly meat bill was negligible and that the consequent savings from her house-keeping money could be stashed away.

Whilst Lizzie was in this mood of near-terminal boredom, she began chatting with one of the hotel guests one Tuesday in the middle of March.

"How's the fishing going, then?" she asked as she pulled a pint of bitter for the guest.

"So, so!" was the reply. "I've caught three or four small ones and just thrown them back. I'm going up the Quinnan again this afternoon for a last session. Perhaps I'll have some better luck. Then it's back to Oban for tomorrow and Thursday, then home on Friday."

Friday! That was the day Ewan went to the Oban meat-market! This had real possibilities!

"And where's home?" asked Lizzie, knowing perfectly well, having snooped in the hotel register, that the fellow was David Wainthorpe from Leeds.

"Leeds. A pretty miserable place to live compared to the west of Scotland. But there's work there, and, after all, we all have to eat!"

Lizzie was not interested in work. But where there is prosperity, there are men with money. She could do all right in somewhere like Leeds!

"A place like Strathquinnan's all right for a holiday, but, if you're not happy living here, it's a bit of a prison." Lizzie sighed theatrically. "If only I could get out!"

"Why don't you then?"

"My man would kill me if I tried to leave. He gets nasty when he's had a few. I've often thought of leaving, but I'd never get clear of the district before he caught up with me and then I'd really be for it!"

"Pity I'm not leaving direct from here. I could have given you a lift to Glasgow, Carlisle or wherever."

"Oh! Mr Wainthorpe. That would have been wonderful. You've no idea how much I hate this place. There's nothing I wouldn't do for the chance of leaving it!"

"Could you get yourself through to Oban on Friday?"

"Aye, but not much before noon and you'd be half-way to Glasgow by then."

"Well, I could wait for you. It would mean stopping overnight somewhere between Oban and Leeds, but I don't start work until Monday so that wouldn't matter."

"Would you wait for me? Oh! You're ever so kind! You've no idea how grateful I am!"

After a few more minutes it was all arranged. Wainthorpe would wait in his car beside the cathedral and Lizzie would join him about noon.

* * * * * *

On the following Friday, Lizzie set out for Oban as usual with her brother-in-law. She had put on her best dress under her raincoat. It was rather light-weight for the time of year, but with over £700 in her hand-bag, she could put up with a little cold until she went on a shopping spree, fitting herself out in all-new clothes. She stuffed as much as she could into a small shoulder bag, not daring to carry anything more conspicuous lest Ewan ask questions. Suppressing her excitement, she chatted easily to Ewan as the van rattled its way along the road to Oban. This would be the last time she travelled in a van. Wainthorpe had a smart new Morris Oxford. That would be her style of transport from now on. In Oban, she left Ewan, arranging to meet up with him about three in the afternoon as usual.

Just before noon, she slipped into the passenger seat of the Morris and by early afternoon, the car was well clear of Oban, heading for Loch Lomond and the south. Early evening found them near Lockerbie where they decided to spend the night.

David Wainthorpe found that a night with Lizzie was a more than adequate compensation for the very minor inconveniences he had suffered in order to help her. However, there was no way he wished to have her company as a long-term relationship. Whilst she was undoubtedly easy on the eye, Wainthorpe had no intentions of giving up his often tempestuous but comfortably predictable marriage of thirteen years, not least because of his three children. However, he need not have worried about getting lumbered with Lizzie. After a few hundred miles in the Morris, she had begun to wonder if she was not destined for something better. Something like Mr McPhail's Rover. Or even the laird's Bentley!

So the two drove south, each wondering how to end this embryonic relationship. Wainthorpe started to extol the virtues of Bradford. Whilst Leeds was good, Bradford would be an ideal place for a new start. Lizzie eagerly grasped the opportunity and soon it was agreed that she would be dropped off in Bradford, an arrangement that suited them both.

It was mid-afternoon on an unseasonably warm March day, when Lizzie strolled through Bradford's main streets. She was hungry, so she decided a nice afternoon tea in a high-class restaurant was what she needed. She found what was obviously just such a place and, judging by the clientele, a very popular one with well-to-do farmers' wives doing their week-end shopping. The place was fairly crowded and she was not too surprised or put about when she realised she would have to share a table. She looked around and spotted a man, early thirties, very well dressed, good-looking in a rugged sort of way, sitting on his own at a table in the corner.

"Do you mind if I join you?" Lizzie asked, with her best smile.

"Delighted, I'm sure." The man rose and drew back a chair for her very politely. His accent was upper-crust Scots, she thought, which was in fact correct. Richard Charles Carmichael had attended one of the minor public schools in Perthshire where he had learned very little but had been given an upper-class veneer which was essential for his chosen profession, womaniser and con-man. These posh restaurants were his happy hunting grounds. Bored wealthy middle-aged women from the prosperous villages and farm-lands of Yorkshire frequented such places and made easy pickings for the intrepid former public school-boy. Some few had complained to the police and, twice, Carmichael had been an unwilling guest of Her Majesty. However, he had learned a lot from those experiences and was now a very careful operator. He waited for Lizzie to open any conversation. He did not have to wait long.

"It's really quite warm for the time of year," said Lizzie.

"Indeed, but one mustn't be deceived into thinking winter's completely over yet. The weather can hold some nasty surprises for us before we're into summer. But no doubt you are well aware of that, coming from Scotland," Carmichael returned with a smile.

"Oh! Is my accent so pronounced?"

"It's delightful. I was at school in Perthshire. Indeed, some of the happiest years of my life were spent in Scotland. I do love to hear that West Highland accent. Do you mind me asking where you're from?"

Lizzie did some quick thinking. "Inverness, but my parents were from the Hebrides so perhaps that's why you detect a trace of the West Highlands."

"My! You are a long way from home! What brings you to Yorkshire? Are you on holiday?"

"No. Sadly my great aunt has died. I've been here to organise the funeral. She had no nearer relatives and so it fell to me to do everything. We were not really very close. I hadn't seen her since I was a wee girl, in fact." Lizzie was improvising furiously, but rather enjoying the experience.

"Oh! I am sorry. It is so sad when older people have no close relatives left. It also makes winding up an estate so much more difficult." Carmichael was anxious now not to sound too interested, but wondered if there might be some rich pickings to be had here.

Lizzie began to fear she might be spinning too ambitious a yarn and so back-pedalled a bit. If she made herself sound fantastically well-off, it might get harder to encourage this chap to pay the bill!

"No, it's not really been too difficult. The old dear had to give up living alone some years ago. She sold her house and I suppose most of her money has gone on nursing home fees. At any rate, all she left was a little in the bank and some rather nice jewellery," Lizzie glanced at her bag which was hanging on the back of her chair.

"Are you staying in Bradford long?"

"No, in fact I only arrived today. You see, my aunt lived in Skipton latterly and I've been staying there. However, I wanted to have a couple of days in Bradford before going back north. I only reached here an hour ago. Now I really must find a hotel. Do you know anywhere you could recommend?"

"When I'm in Bradford, I usually stay in the Carlton. It's not one of the bigger hotels but it suits me. It's not cheap, mind you, but the facilities are good. Every room has its own bath-room, for instance. That's where I'm staying at present, in fact."

This was true. Carmichael had booked in two days earlier when he was in hot pursuit of a middle-aged widow who looked like being an easy touch. However, suddenly her sister had turned up and the two had booked out that morning, leaving Carmichael with nothing to show for his efforts and with a hotel bill he could very well have done without.

Moving into the same hotel as this rather suave and attractive man did seem to open up interesting prospects for Lizzie. Carmichael paid the restaurant bill, insisting on paying Lizzie's as well as his own. A wise investment, he mused to himself.

The afternoon was now well on and Lizzie really should have been buying some clothes to build up her otherwise very scanty wardrobe. However, she did not want to break off contact with this new friend, so the two went together to the hotel.

"By the way, my name's Bernard Christie." It was not, of course, but it was the name Carmichael had registered into the hotel under. "Just so they don't think the wrong thing, my dear, I wonder if we should tell them that you're my married sister? You are married, aren't you?"

Lizzie thought quickly. "I was. My husband was killed in a car crash last year. I'm Irene Dixon." It amused her to assume the first name of the goody-goody girl from the Free Presbyterian Church and to link it with the surname of the Parish minister!

A widow! Better and better! Carmichael thought. Soon Lizzie was installed in a very comfortable first-floor room along the corridor from Carmichael. The two agreed to meet for dinner. After all, what could be more natural than for brother and sister to dine together?

Dinner was a sumptuous and leisurely meal. As the two walked up the rather majestic stair-case, Carmichael said, "I've a bottle of rather nice claret. Would you care for a night-cap?"

Lizzie had only a hazy idea what claret was, but readily agreed. Carmichael brought it to her room and soon Lizzie found herself relaxing in the pleasantly comfortable mellow atmosphere the wine induced. That she would end up in bed with this man, she was taking for granted. Carmichael, would rather have liked that too, but business came first. He slipped a couple of small white pills into Lizzie's third glass of claret. Soon she was out like a light, sleeping too deeply to hear Carmichael pick up her hand-bag and shoulder-bag and quietly leave the room. Carmichael left the hotel, not troubling the proprietor by asking for his account at this late hour, but exiting by a fire-escape at the rear. Three hundred yards away, he reached the car-park where his Austin Healey was waiting. Several miles outside Bradford, he pulled over to examine his winnings. Initial disappointment at finding no jewellery gave way to elation as he drew out a large wad of bank-notes. Not quite the jack-pot, but a very good evening's work! He hid the two bags deep in a thicket by the road-side. Now it was time to move on. Torquay, he thought. Driving all night, he should be comfortably there by morning. It was far enough away from Bradford and sounded the kind of place where he could conduct some more profitable business.

Lizzie woke up with a splitting head-ache. She was lying fully-dressed on the bed. It was already broad-daylight. Slowly she took in her surroundings, her brain stirring into life well behind her body. Carmichael was gone. Her hand-bag was gone and so was her shoulder-bag. Every penny she had was gone, as were what little clothes she had. As

Carmichael had said, the Carlton was not cheap. How she could extricate herself from this place without paying the bill was her next problem. She went downstairs and ate a hearty breakfast. There was no way of knowing when she would next eat. Going to the police would raise all sorts of questions about why she was booked in under an assumed name.

Lizzie asked about the local churches and enquired about the times of the services. Just before eleven, she went out, clad in her rain-coat. The weather had changed overnight. A sleety drizzle was falling and the wind penetrated her light clothing. She started to walk, cursing the fact that Carmichael had taken her only pair of really comfortable shoes with the shoulder-bag, leaving her hobbling on fashionable but uncomfortable stiletto heels. She saw a sign-post for Huddersfield. She must put as much distance between herself and the Carlton as possible. Not having even the price of a bus-fare, there was nothing she could do but walk. The road stretched out ahead of her, long, straight, grey and bleak, its end, almost symbolically, obscured by mist and sleet.

*　　*　　*　　*　　*

Ewan Stewart had waited in Oban for Lizzie until well into the evening, then, unable to think what else to do, he had returned to Strathquinnan. His brother was not due home until the following day so he decided to say nothing about Lizzie's disappearance to anyone. This was a fateful decision. A frantic Alistair spent the Saturday and Sunday searching Oban. On Monday, just as he was opening the butcher's shop, Ewan was approached by two men.

"Mr Ewan Stewart? Could we have a word." There was no real option being offered. Ewan was guided into the shop and the door was locked. "Police," said the older of the two. "You know why we're here. I must tell you that we've dog-teams searching at Duchally. The more helpful you are, the easier it'll be all round. Now what can you tell us?"

Chapter 28

Irene and Shug had fixed their wedding day for the last Saturday of March. They were a very popular couple and the whole village looked forward to the wedding celebrations. The only cloud on the horizon throughout the days prior to the big day was the still unresolved matter of the disappearance of Lizzie Stewart. A sense of dismay and shock permeated every section of society and the finger of suspicion remained resolutely pointed at Ewan. However, the comprehensive searches by the police had turned up no evidence of foul play and the investigation was still proceeding. None of this was going to prevent the wedding going ahead. It did, however, provide enormous scope for gossip.

Everybody in Strathquinnan had a theory about what had happened to Lizzie Stewart. A distinct majority, and certainly not a silent majority, thought that Ewan Stewart knew far more than he was saying. Another group, mainly composed of women who secretly envied Lizzie her good looks and easy popularity with men, held that she must have absconded with some unknown fancy man. A more kindly, but quite unrealistic minority thought she must have been abducted against her will and speculated with awful fascination about what her fate might be. Even fewer could only suggest that she must have slipped off the pier or suffered some other dreadful accident. They gloomily awaited the discovery of her remains washed up on some suitable bleak and desolate shore. Al Stewart did not know what to think, being unable to believe the worst about his own brother, but equally was unwilling to accept that his wife might have deserted him.

The reality for Lizzie was in fact very different from all these scenarios. For three hours she walked through driving rain. Soaked, chilled and miserable, she wondered how much longer she could go on. Her feet were badly blistered and the heel of one of her shoes was working loose. She had left Bradford and was now in relatively open country, unable even to seek some shelter by walking in the lee of buildings. Furthermore, she was unsure of how far it was from Bradford to Huddersfield and totally at a loss as to what to do when she eventually reached there. With any luck, she reasoned, the Carlton Hotel would not realise until the evening at the earliest that she was not coming back. Perhaps they might not notice her absence until the following morning. No doubt the police would be informed. How much manpower they would devote to trying to trace a woman who had skipped without paying her hotel bill, Lizzie had no idea. All she knew was that she wanted to get as far away from Bradford as she possibly could.

She reached a small village as a violent squall lashed her with sleet and hail. She stumbled into the rather inadequate cover provided by a crude bus-shelter. Now she was fighting back tears. Then a car drew up. The window on the passenger side wound down and a kindly faced woman leaned out.

"Eh, lass! You'll have a long wait there. There'll be no buses come along here until morning. We're going to Oldham. Could we drop you somewhere on the way?"

Lizzie had no idea where Oldham was and even less of what towns might lie along the route. However, her wits did not desert her and lies sprang readily to her lips as usual.

"Oldham! That's wonderful! If you would take me, I'd be so glad. I was supposed to meet my brother but somehow I've missed him. Now I want to get to Manchester, so a lift to Oldham would be a great help."

Dimly she remembered that Manchester was somewhere west of Leeds and Bradford, she could only hope that Oldham lay somewhere between the two so that she would not be seen to be talking nonsense. Gratefully she climbed into the back of the car and was soon soaking up the muggy warmth of the interior.

"We'll drop you at the station. You'll be able to get a train into Manchester. Mind you, you may have a bit of a wait. There won't be that many running on a Sunday," the driver said.

"That's all right," replied Lizzie. "I'm just so grateful for a lift. That brother of mine is a right muddle-head. He's probably forgotten all about me."

Later that afternoon, Lizzie alighted at the station, profusely thanking the old couple in the car. She walked confidently into the booking office, but turned and walked out again as soon as they were out of sight. Now what was she to do? At least it had stopped raining although there was still a chill wind which penetrated her inadequate clothing. She walked down the nearly deserted street. With no luggage, not even so much as a handbag, there was no chance of booking in to a hotel without raising all sorts of questions. Apart from that, Lizzie began to realise that she did not want to have to start tomorrow as she had today, as a fugitive fleeing from an unpaid hotel bill. However, there was an urgent need to get a roof over her head for the coming night. And, thinking of urgent needs, it was becoming uncomfortably clear that, to use her late mother's quaint expression, she would soon have to 'spend a penny' and she did not have a penny to her name.

In this frame of mind, uncertain of what to do next, Lizzie walked on past the closed shops, into the suburbs and then into another village. Eventually she came to a well-lit building with an open door. Some kind of church or mission hall, she concluded. Here would be a toilet, warmth and a chance to sit in relative comfort and go over her options. An elderly woman at the door welcomed her warmly. Lizzie coyly explained her immediate pressing need and was escorted to the ladies cloakroom. Several minutes later, a much relieved Lizzie sat demurely in one of the central pews near the back and waited for the evening service to begin. It was deliciously warm and she began to feel increasingly drowsy. If only she could go to sleep, then wake up to find it had all been a dream.

Towards six o'clock, the hall rapidly began to fill with people, many elderly, but with several younger couples with families. By the time the service began, there were few seats left and Lizzie settled down in the comforting anonymity of the crowded building. The sermon was about a story Jesus had told. Some boy had rebelled against his father, had left home and, having spent all his money, was destitute. Coming to his senses, he had decided to go home and risk his father's anger, only to find a warm welcome when he got there. The preacher ended with an impassioned appeal to all who were far from God the Father to repent and return to him. All this was uncomfortably relevant to her, Lizzie realised. Part of her would have liked to have owned up, asked for forgiveness and a chance to start all over again. However, the price was more than she was prepared to pay. She was realist enough to recognise that she would have to confess, not only to God but to her husband. And that would be altogether too humiliating. There had to be another way.

As the congregation stood up for the closing hymn, she knew her time was running out. If only the past would just disappear! If only she could forget her own folly! She still had no plan for the future and she now had only a few minutes before she would be out on the cold and uninviting streets once more. Then suddenly she had an inspiration. There was a way she could make the past disappear!

The service over, the congregation began to disperse, exchanging gossip and farewells as they did so. No one looked at Lizzie as she sat motionless in her seat. The hall cleared and the same elderly woman who had welcomed her at the door began gathering in the hymnbooks. Then she saw Lizzie. She came over and sat down and spoke to her.

"Are you all right, my dear?" she asked anxiously.

Lizzie turned, her mouth slightly open. She gazed vacantly at the woman and said nothing.

Again came the worried question. "Are you all right? You look rather queer. Is it the heat?"

Still Lizzie said nothing, gazing with an unfocused stare in the general direction of the woman but avoiding eye-contact.

Puzzled, the old lady said, "Wait here, my dear. I'll get some help."

A couple of minutes later she returned, along with another younger woman and two men. One sat down in the seat in front of Lizzie and, leaning over the back of the seat, said, "I'm the pastor here, Jim Archer. This is my wife, Mary. Is there something we can do to help you? Can we call a taxi to take you home?"

Lizzie looked blankly in his direction, opened and closed her mouth several times, but said nothing.

"I think we should call a doctor," the second man said. "It looks as though she's suffered some kind of stroke or something. Would you like us to get a doctor?" he asked Lizzie directly.

Staring blankly at him she shook her head. She did not want to have to say anything, but, on the other hand, she did not want to be examined too professionally. The pastor's wife slipped into the pew beside her.

"Why not come home with us and have a nice cup of

tea. Then we can see about getting you home. Can you stand?" She put her hand under Lizzie's elbow and helped her to her feet. "Our house is just round the corner. Come and have a nice cup of tea and then we can see you safely home."

As Mary Archer led Lizzie to the back of the hall, the other three held a hurried conference.

"I still think we should get a doctor, Jim. If she has had a stroke or something, she'll need proper care."

"I'm just not quite sure," said the old lady. "There's something wrong, no doubt, but I don't think it's a medical problem. I get the feeling she's running away from something. Perhaps a brute of a husband. Did you notice she has a wedding ring? Why not see if Dr Conway's in? He's just down the road and if he'd pop in to your house for a cup of tea he could advise and we needn't tell the poor girl he's a doctor at all unless he's sure she's needing treatment."

"Good idea!" said the pastor. "Would you drop in on him on your way home? I'd better go and catch up with Mary. Thanks for the suggestion. Let me know if you don't find him at home, otherwise we'll expect him to drop in later this evening."

The idea of tea was very welcome to Lizzie. She had neither eaten nor had anything to drink since morning. The problem now was that, if she were to keep up her loss-of-memory act and continue to be silent, how was she to convey the message that she really wanted much more than a cup of tea? However, she need not have worried. Soon she was sitting in a small but comfortable living room in front of a blazing fire with a steaming mug of tea cupped in her hands.

From the kitchen came the smell of bacon and toast.

Half an hour later, having had a satisfying supper of fried bacon accompanied by unlimited supplies of toast, Lizzie felt much better. She still had not uttered a word. In some ways she felt guilty, faced with the kindness and concern of the Archers. The temptation to tell the whole unvarnished truth and get it all over and done with was colossal. However, when a girl is both penniless and homeless, she cannot afford the luxury of a sensitive conscience. Later on in the evening, the doorbell rang. An apparently unexpected visitor arrived who was introduced to her as John Conway.

"I'm sorry. What did you say your name was?" asked Dr Conway. Lizzie of course had not said anything and she simply gazed back at him with a vacant look.

More tea was served and the doctor carried a cup across to Lizzie. When she took this in one hand, he promptly offered her scones which she was forced to take with the other. He gazed at her intently and tried to engage her in conversation. Realising she was being tested, Lizzie said nothing.

An hour or so late, Dr Conway left. At the door, he spoke to Jim Archer, "Quite frankly, I don't know what to say. She's not suffered a stroke, or if she has, it's a very mild one. Both her hands are working normally, so there's no paralysis. I am not sure whether she's suffered anything at all. It's possible that she's just on the run from an angry husband or something like that. Alternatively, she could have met with some catastrophic event in life, such as a bereavement, and she's trying to run away from reality. Whatever it is, I think that, if you give her time, it'll sort itself out. I'll drop in tomorrow morning and see how you're coping. Meanwhile, I'll pop into the police station. It's just possible that she's been reported missing but, in my experience, the police don't get all that excited about cases where a mature woman is just trying to get away from a difficult domestic situation. I'm afraid you're saddled with her for the next day or two." This was accompanied by a sympathetic grin.

That night, Lizzie was shown into a small spare bedroom and her hostess provided a night-dress and a towel. Long after the Archers were sound asleep, she lay awake, trying to figure out her next move. At least she had a comfortable and warm bed for the night. She snuggled down gratefully under the covers. What tomorrow might bring, she did not know. Eventually, she decided she would just have to play things by ear, being guided by what others said the following day. So she went to sleep. As it happened, the next day passed uneventfully, with Lizzie spending much of it sitting in a chair by the fire, gazing unseeingly in front of her. The experience was mind-numbingly boring, but until she came up with an alternative strategy, this seemed not just the best, but the only course of action open to her.

That evening John Conway dropped in, once again apparently as a casual visitor. He chatted to Jim Archer about matters related to the mission hall, but once or twice Lizzie became aware that he was watching her intently. That he was some kind of a doctor, she had little difficulty in guessing. He sat down beside her and tried to get her to talk. The conversation, if it can be called a conversation at all, went like this.

"You know, you are going to have to go home soon. What is your address?"

Lizzie looked blank and said nothing.

"What is your name, then?"

"I.....I.....I...don't know." Her eyes welled with tears in the most convincing way, but, then, Lizzie had always been good at turning on the waterworks when it was to her advantage.

"Think! Now what did your mother call you? Throw your mind back. You're a little girl again. Your mum's calling you. What's she saying?"

Lizzie reckoned she could play this game. "Buttons," she said. "She calls me Buttons."

"What about your school-teacher. What did she call you?"

With a convincing burst of tears, Lizzie said repeatedly, "Dumbbell. Dumbbell. That's my name. Dumbbell!"

What he thought of her, she had no way of telling. As he left, he had another confidential chat with Jim Archer.

"There's nothing much wrong with her, possibly nothing at all. Has she said anything?"

"No! You've got more out of her than we have, for what it's worth. Do you think she's just pretending or is she genuine?"

"Terribly difficult to know. As I said on the telephone, the police have had no missing persons reports that might help. On the other hand, if her husband was in the habit of battering her, he might not be in too much of a hurry to contact the police. Another possibility is that she may have come from far away from here. Her accent's certainly not local, possibly not even English, but she's said so little that you can't hope to trace it."

Lizzie was glad of the food and shelter, but bored to tears. How long she could keep this up, she did not know. As long as she said nothing, there was little risk of her giving herself away. What she was sure of was that, at present, she had no alternative, unless she slipped out and started running again. Somehow, that was a very unattractive prospect. She reckoned that if she sat tight, some chance of changing the situation would present itself. The only danger was death by boredom in the meantime!

On the Wednesday, she saw an opportunity. She was sitting listlessly beside the fire when Mary Archer said, "I'm just popping into Oldham. Do you want to come?"

Wordlessly, Lizzie rose, put on her coat and followed her hostess down the road. When they reached the centre of Oldham, Lizzie looked around her, apparently totally bemused.

"This isn't Oban," she said. "Where am I?"

"Oban? Did you say Oban? Why Oban? This is Oldham."

"But you said we were going to Oban. What are we doing in Oldham? I want to go to Oban," and, precisely on cue, the tears ran down her face.

After that, locating Lizzie's origins did not take very

long at all. A telephone call to the police at Oban soon confirmed that they had anxiously been seeking a young woman who answered the description from Oldham. By Friday, Lizzie was getting off the train at Oban, still apparently completely unable to remember a thing about the missing days of her life. She was dreading the return to Strathquinnan and wondered whether she could keep up the amnesia act indefinitely. Fortunately for her, the villagers' attention was taken up with the fact that the very next day Irene and Shug were getting married. The whole community was involved one way or another in the celebrations and so the return of Lizzie attracted much less attention that might otherwise have been the case. Her husband, Al, was puzzled but delighted. He had endured the most anxious week of his life. His relief, however, was completely surpassed by that of his brother Ewan, at last free from suspicion of murder.

Chapter 29

At roughly the same time as Lizzie was alighting from the train at Oban, there was fresh drama for the lifeboat crew at Strathquinnan. There had been elaborate plans for a stag night in the Safe Haven for the bridegroom. Practically all the fishing boats had managed to arrange their sailing schedules so that the crews were at home. There was an open invitation for all the men-folk of the village and its hinterland to gather for a riotous evening at the Safe Haven. However, in the event, most of those who served on the lifeboat were unable to attend. In early afternoon, the maroons were fired and, almost before the echoes had ceased to reverberate around the town, the crew was assembling.

Usually the selection of the lifeboatmen was simply made on the basis of the first five or six suitably qualified men to reach the boathouse went with the cox and the mechanic. This time, for once, Donald McLeod exerted his authority as coxswain and hand-picked his crew, departing from normal practice. Looking round the eleven available men, he nodded to one and another but, when he saw the Fraser brothers, he shook his head.

"Shug! Chick! Not today! We may not be back in time

for the wedding tomorrow. No! No arguing! Neither of you are coming today!"

The two young men were, as might be expected, bitterly disappointed, despite the fact that Donald's decision obviously made very good sense. There were more volunteers for the boat than were required even without the two Fraser brothers and it would be a shame to run the risk of spoiling Irene's big day unnecessarily. So a heavy-hearted Shug and Chick stood on the pier and watched 'Diana' until she disappeared behind Eilean Sgreadan. It was a pleasant spring day with bright sunshine and a gentle breeze blowing in from the south-west, so very different from the conditions in which the boat had put to sea on so many other occasions. The gossip round the shed was that a fishing-boat returning to Mallaig had suffered a fire in the engine room. Apparently the fire was under control, but the vessel had lost all power and was drifting helplessly about six miles off Ardnamurchan. Clearly, there was nothing to worry about. This would be a routine rescue and sometime late in the evening, Strathquinnan could expect to see 'Diana', with the fishing-boat in tow, entering the harbour. So the waiting crowd dispersed.

'Diana' made good time in the calm conditions and, before long, the lifeboatmen could detect a wisp of smoke and steam on the horizon. An hour later and they were alongside the still smouldering boat. The fire was practically extinguished and the immediate danger of her burning to the water-line had clearly passed. However, the situation there was still more serious than they had expected. The fishing-boat was lying very deep in the water. Some of this was no doubt due to the hundreds of gallons of water the crew had used to bring the fire under control. However, the problem was not wholly explained by that. She was obviously still taking in water somewhere. Possibly a soldered joint on the engine cooling system had melted in the fierce heat and sea-water was steadily flowing into her. To make matters worse, her bilge-pumps had packed up.

A portable pump was hurriedly transferred from the lifeboat and soon a reassuring gush of water from its hose indicated that it was working well. Donald decided to evacuate three of the five fishermen to the safety of the lifeboat and to wait until the pump had had time to reduce the water in the other craft before attempting a tow. The fishing-boat was wallowing sluggishly and, not only would it be a heavy tow, but it might be so unstable as to abruptly overturn and sink, dragging 'Diana' with it. The weather was set fair, so there was no anxiety among the two crews as they settled down to wait. As the afternoon wore on, there was little other activity on the water. The ferry from Coll and Tiree passed several miles away to the south on its return journey to Oban. Farther out in the Minch three or four trawlers were returning north-ward to Mallaig. A Russian trawler, easily recognised by its rusty hull and complex radio-masts, lay a couple of miles away. The barometer reading was high, so, if the lifeboat had to sit it out all night, there was no cause for concern.

The pump appeared to be struggling to keep pace with the water entering the fishing-boat's hull. However, after an hour, there was a visible improvement, so the water leaving the boat was clearly considerably more than was entering it. Despite this, for safety's sake, Donald decided to hove to for another couple of hours or so. There would still be plenty of daylight hours left and by then the other boat should then be floating much higher in the water. Gradually, however, a sea-mist developed, cutting visibility to a mile or so. The Russian boat disappeared from view as the mist gradually wrapped itself round the two boats. Soon visibility was down to less than a quarter of a mile. However, that was more than adequate to ensure there would be no risk of collision. There was very little shipping in these waters at any time and a visual watch was probably all that was required. Just to make doubly safe, however, and as a precaution, Donald decided to maintain a radar watch and deputed two of the crew to take turns at the set. Two others were put on a visual watch on deck.

Tam, doing his stint on the radar, watched the monotonous sweep on the screen. The mainland at Ardnamurchan was easily recognised to the east. The blip of the Russian craft was equally easily picked out to the west. The other Mallaig-bound boats were presumably that scatter on the screen far to the north. Tam found it hard to concentrate on the rather monotonous screen that flickered in front of him. Gradually the distant scatter of the Mallaig boats disappeared and the rest of the afternoon slipped by uneventfully. Then Tam suddenly woke up to the fact that a small blip had detached itself from the Russian one and was heading their way. He called Donald over.

"Looks very small," said the cox. "A dinghy or something similar. It should soon be visible. I think the mist is beginning to lift."

It was indeed. He stood upright, peering through the all-pervading whiteness. A few minutes later, a low, grey shape appeared over quarter of a mile away. He grabbed his glasses and saw a small boat with two men in it, rowing furiously towards them. It took only five more minutes to come along side. As soon as it was in hailing distance, one of the men shouted, "Asylum! Asylum! We want political asylum!"

"Funny," muttered Dod, "not one of them could speak English when we wanted help from them!"

"I have no authority to offer you asylum," shouted Donald. "This is a lifeboat, not a Naval craft and not owned by the British Government. Come alongside and I'll radio for instructions."

"Please don't do that! Our ship will pick up your broadcast and then they'll come after us. It's life or death for us, certainly. What they might do with you, I don't know!"

"A pretty problem, this," said Donald to Dod and Tam, the two who were standing nearest to him. "We're almost ready to tow that boat, but the best speed we'll make with it in tow will be about four knots. The commies will do three times that and be alongside in minutes. A great deal depends on how long it takes them to miss our two friends here." He nodded at the two men, anxiously waiting in their craft as it bobbed up and down alongside the lifeboat.

Meanwhile the mist was clearing fast and the Russian

vessel was just visible as a darker grey smudge against the all-pervading whiteness. In seconds, its shape became more distinct, a sinister dark ship made more ominous by the strands of mist still wreathing her upper-works. Suddenly a puff of smoke belched from the distant trawler's funnel.

"I think that's your answer," said Dod. "They're getting under way. It's decision time!"

Donald hurriedly decided. "The RNLI's job is to save lives at sea. We'll abandon the fishing boat here. We can safely leave the pump running. She may be saved yet, but, meanwhile, we had better make a run for it. That trawler would soon catch up with us in the open sea but, if we can make it to shallow waters, we may be able to stay out of her reach. Cast off!"

Without further delay, the two Russians were hauled aboard. The twin engines were throbbing and the mooring-ropes were released. At full throttle, 'Diana' surged forward. She heeled over as she swung eastwards and headed for the nearest land, a group of low-lying islands off the main-land coast. Donald urgently radioed, reporting the situation to the coastguards. He anxiously looked at the Russian vessel which was now under way and swinging round in their direction, throwing up an impressive bow-wave.

"It'll be touch and go," he muttered. "We might just make it to the shallows. They must be making thirteen or more knots to our nine."

The radio crackled and he took a message. He turned round to his anxious friends. "The nearest ship is a fishery-protection boat out of Stornoway. She's making her best speed, but she'll not be here until well after mid-night. The RAF is sending a plane. Much good that'll be!"

As the islands grew larger to the east, so did the spy-ship to the west. As Donald had said, it would be touch and go. The gap between the two craft narrowed to a quarter of a mile and a voice in good English shouted on a loud-hailer for the life-boat to heave to. Ignoring it, Donald steered for a gap in the islands.

"The tide's on the ebb," he said. "We should have just enough water to get through and there's then no chance of them following. Their ship draws far too much. They'll have to launch boats if they want to keep up the chase but I wouldn't worry too much about that. We can then play hide and seek with them among the islands until the fishery protection boys get here."

He looked anxiously at the chart and at the depth-sounder. Although the gap he was heading for was only a couple of hundred yards away, 'Diana' was still in eight fathoms. Donald knew, however, that the bottom shoaled very steeply and that, according to the chart, there was a mere fathom, six feet, of water between the islands. That was if you believed the chart. However, the depths round this part of the coast kept changing as the sand was either scoured away or deposited by the currents. There was serious risk that there might be ample depth for the pursuer to chase through the gap or, alternatively, insufficient depth for the lifeboat. The depth-guage was now showing the depth decreasing rapidly. At six fathoms, Donald adjusted the setting on the instrument to read in feet. 30....25....20....15....10. The bottom was coming up alarmingly. Donald would have loved to shut down the throttles and creep through, but with the Russian now only two hundred yards away, he pressed on at full speed. 9.... 8.... 7.... 6. Then it seemed to hold steady at six. The Russian vessel was now slowing down. The steeply shoaling bottom was obviously worrying her captain. The gap between the two craft started to widen once more. Then, just when the lifeboatmen thought they were through, 'Diana' juddered abruptly to a halt. Dod pulled back the throttles. Gingerly, he put the engines astern, gradually increasing the power until the whole boat was shuddering under the battle between the fast-revolving propellers and the tenacious grip of the muddy sea-bed. It soon became all too obvious that the lifeboat had driven herself hard into the soft ground below the keel.

"Look's as though we're well and truly stuck," said Tam, stating the obvious. "When's low tide?"

"About eight. It'll be nearly eleven before we can get off. The only consolation is that our friends over there can't come any nearer."

A rattle of an anchor chain confirmed that the trawler was not going to try to close the gap. However, there was soon much frantic activity on the deck of the Russian ship.

"They're going to launch a boat! What do we do now?" muttered Dod. Donald, however, was already radioing the latest developments to the coastguard. The reply was that the expected time of arrival of the RAF was four minutes.

"They can hardly bomb the commies out of the water,

so I don't know what good they think they can do," said Donald, as he watched the large ship's boat being lowered down the side of the trawler. He picked up his glasses.

"Seven men," he reported. "At least two have rifles." A small motor crackled into life and the boat swung round towards them.

"Shall I shoot a flare at them," asked Dod, the flares ready beside him.

"No! For any sake, don't! We don't want to start World War Three just yet!"

"You're not just going to hand those poor devils over to them?"

Before Donald could answer, a rumble like thunder re-echoed round the islands and a sleek fighter-plane swept in over the hills to the east and roared over both craft.

"Hawker Hunter!" said Tam knowledgeably, as the

jet soared back into the sky. The Russian boat hesitated for a minute, but only for a minute. Then it started to chug towards them again. The Hunter meanwhile had climbed high to the west and was wheeling round. It came screaming down towards the two boats. At one hundred feet, the noise of machine-guns cracked out, and the narrow stretch of water between the boats seemed to boil. The fighter made a tight turn to the east and swung round again, this time lining up on the Russian boat. Awe-struck, the Strathquinnan men watched. The man at the tiller of the Russian boat swung his helm hard over and the boat started to swing round. The Hunter passed overhead at less than fifty feet, its slip-stream rippling the waves, its jet engines practically deafening Scot and Russian alike.

"Great!" exclaimed Donald. "Enough fire-power there to make them think twice! I think they'll get the message all right!"

The Hunter was lining up for a third pass, but by this time the Russian boat was headed straight for its mother ship. After a few more minutes, a second RAF plane appeared, high above the first. The two circled for a few minutes, then the first made a low pass over the life-boat, waggling its wings before disappearing over the hills beyond. The second plane descended to about five hundred feet and lazily circled for some twenty minutes before it, in turn, was relieved by a third. So the RAF kept a perpetual presence over the lifeboat.

Meanwhile the tide continued to ebb, leaving 'Diana' all the more helplessly marooned. Daylight was now failing and, with the darkness, a new worry crept over the

Strathquinnan men. Would the Russians mount an assault under cover of darkness? However, in the fading light, they saw the rays of the setting sun reflected from the fuselage of a much larger plane to the north and soon they heard, mingling with the noise of the jet air-craft, the comfortingly familiar sound of a Shackleton, its four mighty Griffin piston engines giving out a World War 2 sound. The huge aircraft established a figure of eight circling pattern of flight a thousand feet or more above the jet.

So the evening wore on, with the Hunters coming and going, each doing its spell of watch before being relieved by the next. It was a moonless night and eventually the Russian ship disappeared totally in the murk. When the darkness was complete, the sound of oars could be heard from the direction of the trawler. Hurriedly Donald radioed a report. Then, suddenly, the whole scene was illuminated as the Shackleton released a parachute flare. Caught by its light was the Russian ship's boat, half-way between the trawler and the lifeboat. Almost before the Russians had time to react, the Hunter screamed down upon the scene, its guns chattering. Again the sea boiled. Again the Russians retreated. The Shackleton continued its majestic sweep, dropping flares at regular intervals to keep the whole area illuminated.

As the night wore on, 'Diana' became more upright with the rising tide lifting her from the juicy mud. By eleven, she was afloat, but Donald decided to anchor where they were. There was now no compelling reason to venture into the shallow waters between the islands with all the attendant risks of running aground once more. At about one in the morning, there appeared the lights of a ship far out at sea. The Russians now decided that a discreet withdrawal was called for and the noise first of its anchor chain, then of its engines could just be heard over the ever-present rumble of the two planes above. With no riding lights showing, the trawler slipped away to the south-west.

"She won't get far," remarked Dod. "The fishery protection ship will soon run her down."

"I don't think so," replied Donald. "I think they'll just let them go. With East-West relations the way they are, no one wants to provoke a diplomatic incident. On balance, the West has won this round. Those two," he nodded towards the two asylum-seekers, "will no doubt earn their freedom with a lot of valuable intelligence gen."

'Diana' was free now to move into deeper water and, because of the softness of the bottom that had so effectively held her prisoner, she appeared to be completely undamaged. Slowly, Donald took her back to open sea. The watchful Shackleton had now climbed to several thousand feet, but still maintained vigil high above, her engines comfortingly droning incessantly and her navigation lights reassuringly visible. A radio message came requesting that 'Diana' make for Mallaig and hand the two Russians over to the police there. This was a disappointment to the Strathquinnan men who would much rather have returned direct their own base to be in good time for the wedding. However, as Mallaig was a railway town and, no doubt a strong escort was already being sent there to take the Russians south, they fell in with this request.

Chapter 30

David McPhail stood at the end of the pier, looking out over a calm but empty sea. He felt somewhat over-dressed for his surroundings, wearing, as he was, his very best suit and sporting a crimson carnation in the button-hole. However, the explanation was simple. This was Irene and Shug's wedding day and the service was scheduled for noon at the little Free Presbyterian Church. The day had dawned bright and almost unseasonably warm, excellent weather for the day's festivities. However, McPhail knew that the only cloud on Irene's horizon was that she had set her heart on having a guard of honour made up of all the lifeboat crew and there was still no sign of the 'Diana'. Nor was there clear information to be had about what was going on. There had been much speculation in the village overnight, but no reliable news.

Even in his privileged position, McPhail knew very little. He had been listening to the radio messages and making frequent telephone calls here and there, but still what reports he had were shrouded in mystery. What was clear was that the Strathquinnan men had been at risk from Russian trawlermen but were now all safe and well. What was strange was the absence of any real detail in the news bulletins from the coastguards and police. Wild theories abounded and hard facts were scarce. Something unusual was happening, that was clear, but no one seemed to know quite what.

As noon drew closer, David McPhail looked anxiously at his watch and whispered a prayer to the Christ he had come to know so much better since that memorable experience in the church last Christmas. Then he hurried up the street, just managing to reach the little church before the bride arrived. He slipped into a back pew and again prayed that the lifeboat would be back in time. For once, he was grateful for the long-windedness of the Free Presbyterian Church. If the service dragged on long enough, the boat might be back before it was over.

Only five minutes late, the blushing bride arrived and the ceremony began. David tried to concentrate, but all the time his thoughts kept slipping back to the lifeboat and its crew. The minister was reading from the Psalms in the gentle lilt of the Northwest Highlands.

'Bless the Lord, O my soul, and forget not all his benefits; who redeemeth thy life from destruction; who crowneth thee with loving kindness and tender mercies.'

How appropriate that seemed, thought McPhail as he looked forward at the erect figures of the bridegroom and the best man. Those two brothers had been perilously close to destruction several times in the few years McPhail had known them. He had always recognised the dangers but the stark reality of the hazards these men again and again had willingly faced were accentuated in his mind by the Broughty Ferry experience. Dragging his thoughts back from the sad memories of that other church over on the east coast and of that heart-breaking service there last December, he tried to concentrate again as the minister read on.

'He hath not dealt with us after our sins; nor rewarded us according to our iniquities. For as the heaven is high above the earth, so great is his mercy toward them that fear him.'

That certainly seemed very personally relevant to McPhail as he thought back over the recent weeks and reflected on the deep sense of peace with God and of being forgiven that he now enjoyed.

'The mercy of the Lord is from everlasting to everlasting upon them that fear him.'

But where, Oh where, was the lifeboat? The bride looked so radiant and serene, thought McPhail. Yet he knew how much she wanted the rest of the crew to be there to share her happiness. So the service proceeded. It was still going on when 'Diana' slipped round the west end of Eilean Sgreador and entered harbour. In record time, she was made fast and the crew legged it up the cobbled street, arriving at the church just as the doors opened. Irene and Shug, or, more precisely, Mr and Mrs Hugh Fraser emerged, to pass between two lines of breathless, unshaven, grimy, tired, but supremely happy men.

At the back of the crowd which formed a wide semicircle at the church door stood David McPhail, trying to hide the fact that his eyes were glistening with tears of joy and gratitude. An enormous feeling of pride and thankfulness surged through him as he reflected on the great privilege that had been his to be associated with such men as these and to know he belonged in a community like Strathquinnan.